"You invented a lover to keep me at bay?"

"Does it really matter?" Linsey was too anxious about getting home to Sean to concentrate on what Jarvis was saying. Then suddenly she felt the boat moving. She rushed toward the door.

When he caught her arm, bringing her to an abrupt halt, she aimed her open hand at his cold hard face. But it didn't land, and he held her easily until she finished struggling and slumped against him, defeated.

"That's better," he said almost mildly. "I take it you're so keen to get home you're ready to jump overboard?"

"Yes." Her prayer was a harsh whisper. "Oh, Jarvis, please." Her face was stark white; her eyes implored him beseechingly. What did her pride matter? It was Sean who counted. "I'll do anything."

"Will you?" he asked. "Anything?"

MARGARET PARGETER

not far enough

Harlequin Books

TORONTO • NEW YORK • LOS ANGELES • LONDON
AMSTERDAM • PARIS • SYDNEY • HAMBURG
STOCKHOLM • ATHENS • TOKYO • MILAN

Harlequin Presents first edition October 1982
ISBN 0-373-10540-1

Original hardcover edition published in 1982
by Mills & Boon Limited

CHAPTER ONE

THE man stood motionless on the deck of the large yacht which lay at anchor far out in the bay. This was the second morning Jarvis Parradine had stood there. The spot was idyllic, but he was aware that his crew was curious. They knew him as a man possessed of a curious restlessness who, unless he was working, rarely stayed in the same place longer than twenty-four hours.

He stared towards the distant island, set like a jewel amid the beauty of the Indian Ocean, narrowing his eyes against the shimmer of early morning sunlight on the water. The girl was on the beach again. He recognised that she was the same one because of the dress she wore and the way in which her long hair whipped about her small head in the wind. Only one girl he had ever known had hair like that and a certain distinctive something to the set of her slender neck and shoulders.

Drawing a deep breath, he reached for his binoculars—German ones, with some of the world's most powerful lenses. He hadn't used them yesterday, to put an end to his morbid uncertainty. He had felt like a child with a present, afraid to open it for fear it didn't contain what he had hoped and prayed for. He had spent the rest of the day thinking, and his thoughts had been hard and cruel, lashed with a driving urge for revenge. A bitter sense of anticipation had kept him awake for most of the night, bringing him up on deck with the dawn. Long ago he had given up all hope of finding her. Now hope was alive again, but it brought him no pleasure. If it really was Linsey, he would see that she suffered, if it was the last thing he ever did!

Lifting the binoculars at last, he studied the lone figure. She came in focus, suddenly so close she might have been standing directly in front of him. His breath rasped and his face paled, but otherwise he might have been carved out of stone. Putting the binoculars down again, he called grimly for a deckhand to lower a dinghy.

The sea was a wonderful translucent blue and the air refreshingly cool at such an early hour. Linsey watched it moodily, without really seeing it. Mauritius was always beautiful, both scenically and weather-wise, but this morning she was almost too tired to appreciate it. That she could find no logical reason for feeling so tired didn't make her feel any happier. Why, after such a long period of relative tranquillity, should her life be turned suddenly upside down again? It didn't seem fair. Linsey's blue eyes clouded as she thought of the problems which now beset her.

Putting her hands over her face, she sighed, trying futilely to block out mental pictures. It hadn't been easy to leave Jarvis and come here, but slowly and painfully, with Harriet's help, she had learnt to accept that she would never see her husband again. When she had first arrived on the island, she had been ill and distraught, unable to think clearly. When she had recovered a little, she had been anxious to at least let Jarvis know where she was. But by this time Sean had been well on the way and she had heeded Harriet's warning that while Jarvis might not want a reconciliation, he might want his child. He could easily take her baby from her when it arrived. This had thrown Linsey into such a blind panic, she had immediately changed her mind about getting in touch with him. After all, Jarvis had only himself to blame that she had left him, and she daren't run the risk of having to part with her baby. She had listened to Harriet, respecting her wider experience.

From that moment Linsey had never allowed herself to even consider contacting Jarvis again. He wouldn't want her back, she had decided bitterly, glad that she had had the sense to follow Harriet's advice rather than her own inclinations. He had married her, taking advantage of the fact that she was only eighteen. Then, after being unkind to her, he had finally rejected her for another woman. Within two months of returning from their brief honeymoon, hadn't she found him in his office kissing a well-known actress? But that had been the final blow, not the first one. Many things had culminated to so affect Linsey's state of mind that she had finally run away. The whole situation had proved too much for her to cope with, and she had been too young to think of any other solution.

Over three years now stretched between Sean's birth and the present day. Linsey was twenty-two, over four years older, and although she considered herself better equipped to deal with emergencies, she had never visualised anything quite as bad as the one she was faced with now.

Harriet had died, ten days ago, after a long illness from which her doctor had fully expected her to recover. Her sudden death had been a shock, and not until then had Linsey realised how exhausted she had become from nursing her. Since Harriet's death she had been more than grateful for the continuing help she had received from Musetta, Sean's young nursemaid. Musetta had stayed and carried on with her duties, although there was little money now to pay her. At the end of the last week Linsey had managed to give her something, but she doubted if there would be anything more.

Musetta slept at the cottage and would be there when Sean woke up, otherwise Linsey couldn't have left him. There had been an urgent desire in her to leave her bed and come down to the shore, to walk there alone for a change, without an over-intelligent three-year-old who demanded all her attention. Always she had loved this time of day, before the rest of the world was awake, but never more so than now, when only the early mornings seemed able to provide the tranquillity she was so desperately in need of.

Moving her slender shoulders, as though trying to ease the strain of the past weeks, she failed to see the man approaching until he was nearly on her. This part of the island was quiet, and the cottage where she lived stood on its own at the end of a village. Tourists came here occasionally, but found little to incite their interest. The area, however, was never completely deserted. Those who didn't work in the hotels or on the sugar plantations often ran a small business of their own, while the elderly wandered the streets and talked or sat dreaming in one of the many sun-drenched corners, with their grandchildren playing at their feet. Linsey certainly had no reason to feel alarmed at the sound of a footstep.

It wasn't until a voice spoke her name that she spun around, as if she had been shot.

'Jarvis!' Her eyes lit with terror, widening with shock. Her face, pale from spending too much time indoors nursing Harriet, flushed, then went white. She stepped back, away from him, staring at him as though he was some fearful spectre. 'No!' she whispered hoarsely, swaying on her feet. 'No, it can't be!'

Jarvis Parradine smiled. It wasn't a smile so much as a mere twist of his lips. 'You seem surprised to see me, Linsey,' he said softly.

The very smoothness of his tones made her shiver. Dazed, her eyes rested on his lean, handsome face, as she made an unconscious effort to pull herself together. He hadn't changed a great deal. The lines on his face were deeper, especially round his eyes and mouth, but this was to be expected in a man of almost thirty-eight.

It couldn't have anything to do with her running away from him, and, if anything, they added to, rather than detracted from, his distinguished good looks. His eyes were bleaker than she remembered, his mouth held more tightly, yet she sensed that despite his harsh demeanour he was trying not to frighten her too much. Why? she wondered wildly. Jarvis had never been the most tolerant of men, and hadn't she, in leaving him, committed one of the most unforgivable of crimes?

'It—it's been a long time,' she stammered, her heart beating like a drum under the thin material of her dress.

'Yes,' he agreed softly, his eyes glinting, 'it has been a long time.'

Why didn't he shout and rave at her? It wouldn't have made her feel half as uneasy as this guarded, indifferent approach. Even his eyes were expressionless, as if he was determined to give nothing away. Yet what could he be trying to hide? she asked herself. Hatred—contempt? Certainly not love. Surely he could have no feeling of any kind left for her, not after all these years.

Unable to find the answer to such questions, she enquired unevenly, 'How did you get here?'

'My yacht,' he replied briefly.

'Your yacht,' she reiterated stupidly, too stunned by reaction to take this in. 'But how did you know where to find me?'

'I didn't,' he drawled, the first hint of derision creeping into his voice. 'You didn't really think I'd still be looking for you, did you? You could say I was passing by and happened to see you on the beach.'

Linsey trembled as his anger flicked her, but tried not to let him see. Why hadn't fate looked kindly on her, for a change, and kept her at home this morning? Fear tightened her throat as this reminded her of Sean, and she went cold all over. It was essential that Jarvis should never find out about Sean, not when everything was over between them. Jarvis had always been arrogant, stiff with pride, and people rarely changed much. He would never take her back now, but there was still a chance that he would want his son.

Trying to give herself time to think, she asked unsteadily, 'Did you ever look for me?'

'Yes,' he replied, so unemotionally she might have been a misplaced book, 'occasionally I have done.'

He talked as if he had only searched for her when he had nothing better to do. Again, as another thought struck her, Linsey bit her lip fiercely. 'Now that you've found me I expect you'll want a divorce?'

His eyes hardened. 'I could have divorced you before now for desertion.'

Inside, all the heat churning through her froze. 'Why didn't you, then?'

'I never got round to it,' he snapped.

Somehow she couldn't take this for an answer. 'Why not?' she persisted.

His eyes were busy going over her again and he replied mockingly, 'Perhaps because I haven't yet met another woman I wanted to marry. Or it could be that my first experience of matrimony has put me off completely. And not all women demand a wedding ring before allowing me the pleasure of their company.'

On a ragged breath, Linsey dragged her wide eyes from his to gaze down at the sand. It lay silvery white, half covering her feet, so still and smooth while her whole world rocked about her. 'I'm sure there have been other women,' she muttered, recalling the last time she had seen him, 'women who could satisfy you. I didn't have enough experience.'

'You had none at all,' he agreed cruelly. 'But you weren't doing so badly, I suppose, for a beginner. In fact, you were distinctly promising,' he reminisced dryly, 'before you decided you'd had enough and walked out.'

Colour crept painfully into Linsey's pale cheeks and she clenched her hands. How could he say this when they had been married less than three months, and, because of—of everything, had actually lived together as man and wife less than two weeks?

'That's all in the past,' she whispered hoarsely, unable to dwell on it for more than seconds, and she was shocked that even such a brief recall could still make her heart leap. It must be the remembered trauma of disillusionment, it could be nothing else. 'It's too late,' she declared bitterly, 'to begin again.'

'Who said anything about beginning again?' he taunted contemptuously, his eyes cold as they rested on her uncertain face.

Linsey flinched, trying to stop herself from staring at him so closely. Why was it that while she hated him, her eyes almost refused to leave him? 'I'm sorry,' she paused, swallowing a peculiar lump in her throat, 'I put that the wrong way. What I meant to say was . . .' again for unknown reasons she hesitated, 'I'll agree to a divorce if you'll arrange it.'

'There's no hurry,' he surprised her by answering, his voice grating coldly. 'After all, what's a few more weeks after so many years? Over four years, hasn't it been, Linsey?'

She could have told him to the day, but she merely nodded. 'I suppose you'll want to finish your holiday first?'

'I want to finish my holiday, yes,' he agreed.

Her nerves taut, Linsey asked, trying to sound as if it didn't matter, 'You'll be leaving here immediately?'

'Oh, I don't think so,' deliberately, it seemed, he echoed her note of cool carelessness, 'I have a sudden fancy to remain on Mauritius a little longer. You're living here, I take it?'

'Yes.' This time her voice was a strangled whisper.

'Then we might manage to renew our—er—acquaintance,' he suggested crisply. 'We have things to talk over, and no other form of communication is ever quite as satisfactory.'

Panic struck her so sharply she almost cried out. Whatever happened, Jarvis mustn't stay here, yet she felt his will like an avalanche of steel, knocking aside her terrified protests before she had even time to voice them. He appeared, on the surface, to be calm and reasonable, so why did she suspect this was merely a blind? That, so far as she was concerned, he would be entirely without mercy? But the impression was fleeting. Sanity returned to assure her she must be mistaken. 'For you to stay here would be a waste of time, Jarvis.'

'Why?'

'Surely that's obvious?'

He frowned, as though nothing was that obvious to him. Linsey wished he would stop staring at her, having no idea, as the sun struck her small, exotic features, how beautiful she looked. The sunlight, so illuminating on her face, could reveal no flaw in a skin so fine it might have been fashioned from rose petals, while not even the shabbiness of her dress could disguise the perfection of her slender curves. Ignoring her last observation, Jarvis said, 'You don't look a day older, Linsey.'

An odd note in his voice disturbed her faintly, renewing her uneasiness. She didn't take his cynical remark as any kind of compliment and retorted bitterly, 'I am older, though, in lots of ways.'

'I should hope so,' he replied coldly. 'Only children run away from their problems. You aren't planning to disappear again, are you?'

As she considered him uncertainly, something of her inner confusion was reflected in her huge, apprehensive eyes. She had beautiful eyes of a soft violet blue, a colour impossible to describe accurately, with lashes so thick and curling they looked tangled. 'Why should I run away again?' she queried, knowing she might have to. Only this time it might not be so easy, with a three-year-old boy to hamper her.

'I never knew why you did so in the first place,' he said grimly, his eyes chips of green ice.

'I'm sure you must have had a very good idea!' she cried resentfully. For the life of her she couldn't bring herself to mention, in so many words, having caught him in his office with Olivia James in his arms. That would smack too much of jealousy, an emotion she still refused to recognise. What she had felt then had been the overwhelming despair of the betrayed, nothing more or less.

Again he frowned, his glance probing, as if trying to read her mind. 'I had a vague idea that everything was getting too much for you, but I still don't believe anything was bad enough to justify your leaving me. For over four years I haven't known whether you were dead or alive.'

'I left a note.'

'Just to say you weren't coming back—remarkable only for its briefness. The usual type of note, I imagine, wives leave for husbands who fall short of impossible expectations.'

'You—you didn't try very hard,' she choked, able to recall, even now, the chill of his increasing indifference.

The first visible signs of unleashed fury showed on his hard face. 'Perhaps my experience with girls of your tender age was too limited,' he ground out. 'I realised afterwards that the whole situation, from the death of your parents on our honeymoon to your losing the baby, was fraught with danger, yet you solved nothing by taking the coward's way out and running away.'

As a strangled cry inadvertently escaped her and she

turned from him abruptly, his eyes darkened harshly. 'I'm sorry. Does the memory of losing the baby still upset you so much? Didn't you realise it would have been perfectly possible to have another?'

A guilty flush stained Linsey's averted cheeks and she knew he must see it. How could she confess she hadn't lost the baby, after letting him believe she had? And she had known she hadn't lost it, even before she had left him. Wasn't that what she had gone to his office to tell him? Hadn't she hoped that the news might make everything all right, only to find him making love to Olivia James? All the same, many would say she had acted unforgivably in keeping such information from him. They would consider, as it was his child, that he had the right to know. Was it a feasible excuse that she had only been eighteen and very frightened, as much by her own emotions as anything else? She had been convinced that the love in their marriage was only on her side. How many times had she agonised over it? Jarvis had been loving, but never once had he actually told her that he loved her. He had hinted, perhaps, and lusted after her body, which, she had come slowly to realise, was not quite the same thing.

Helplessly she swung back to him, shaking her head. 'I'd rather not talk about it,' she muttered hurriedly. 'What's the use of raking up the past when we've been so long apart? If you let me have the papers, or whatever, about the divorce, I'll sign anything . . .'

'Will you?' His voice was deceptively mild. 'You seem extremely obliging of a sudden, which somehow I find difficult to believe. Once you appeared to take pleasure in opposing me in just about everything. You were as contrary as the devil, too. You didn't seem to want the baby, then you refused to be consoled when you lost it.'

Why didn't he stop tormenting her? A breathless feeling swept over her like a tidal wave. How dared he mention that? She had been very young and hadn't known a thing. On their wedding night, she had merely suggested they should wait a while before starting a family. But Jarvis had only laughed—laughed and declared that that was one of the main reasons why he had married her, for a son. With a determined glint in his eyes he had swept her up in his arms and carried her through to their bedroom.

That had been the beginning of their honeymoon, the start of their life together, and she didn't want to be reminded of it in any way. Her skin burned, whereas before it had merely been hot, as she recalled her own awakening response to his passion. 'I've told you,' she gasped, 'I've changed!'

'It might be interesting to discover how much,' he jibed enigmatically.

'It would be senseless when we're talking about a divorce,' she said sharply.

'Of course,' he agreed silkily. 'How right you are. I expect you'll want alimony?'

Bleakly Linsey reflected that she could certainly do with some money of some kind. Since Harriet had died, and her income with her, she had worried continually about the future. How was she to make ends meet? Yet, considering everything, how could she possibly take anything from Jarvis?

'No, thank you, I can manage,' she assured him stiffly.

'Can you?' he asked narrowly. 'How? How do you manage?'

'Oh, there are ways and means,' she replied cautiously, unable at the moment to think of any.

'Such as?' he prompted smoothly, his eyes glinting as they rested on her clenched hands. 'Are you living with someone? Perhaps another man?'

'You—you could say that.' Linsey felt hysterical laughter welling in her throat and made a desperate effort to subdue it. Jarvis couldn't know she was thinking of their three-year-old son.

'So that's it!' With apparent indifference Jarvis turned his back so that she didn't see the anger which changed his face to a chiselled mask. When he swung around again his eyes were blank. 'It's certainly no surprise to learn that you aren't living alone. Not when I recall the way you were shaping, at least, on our honeymoon.'

'You're insulting and mistaken!' she began hotly, forgetting she had condemned herself by her own devious confession.

'Who are you trying to fool, Linsey?' he cut in curtly, evidently with no intention of sparing her feelings. 'You knew nothing when I married you. I'd say your wedding night was more of a shock than anything else, but until something about me began putting you off you seemed to enjoy that side of our marriage well enough.'

'It wasn't you,' she stammered unhappily.

'It was certainly something,' he snapped. 'You blew hot and cold until I was nearly out of my mind. First you didn't want me, then you'd make a damned nuisance of yourself, when I was busy.'

She flinched from his humiliating remarks, her cheeks flushed with indignation. 'I didn't expect you to be absorbed with business on our honeymoon . . .'

'There was a merger going through, you knew that. I had to keep in constant touch with London.'

'Perhaps I was only trying to please you.'

He shrugged, his mouth twisting. 'Were you? Well, it doesn't matter now. What matters now is that I remember how much you enjoyed sex—when you felt like it! Enough to convince me you wouldn't give it up so easily.'

Uncertainly Linsey lowered her eyes, trying painfully to concentrate on that short period of her life.

She was disconcertingly aware that Jarvis could still make her heart race just by looking at her, but it was difficult to recall exactly how she had felt on their honeymoon. Drawing a sharp breath, she remembered how he could make her feel. He had been an expert in the art of seduction. Her own responses, after four years, were a little hazy, but she did know that for a long time after coming here she had ached for him—so much so that eventually she had had to force herself to stop thinking of him. 'You must think what you like,' she whispered, every nerve in her body strung tight.

Coldly, Jarvis lashed out at her again. 'What on earth made you come here in the first place? I could have sworn you had no boy-friends in London.'

She stepped back, as though his contempt struck her like a physical blow. 'A friend of my mother's lived here. She was the only person I could think of.'

'Really?' His voice was laced with sarcasm. 'Where is she now? Or did you desert her in favour of this boy-friend?'

'No, she died.' Linsey didn't say when.

Jarvis didn't appear to want to know. His eyes smouldering, he snapped, 'I presume she knew about our marriage, that you'd run out on it, for the want of a little courage?'

'She knew I'd been married, yes,' Linsey murmured thinly, ignoring the rest.

'Didn't she advise you to get in touch with me?' he asked harshly.

'No,' Linsey faltered, 'I don't think so.'

'My God!' he said savagely, 'what sort of woman was she? Or,' his eyes narrowed into glittering slits, 'was the story you told her so totally condemning that she imagined you'd had a fortunate escape from a fate worse than death?'

Because it was so near the mark, Linsey flushed with guilt again. Rather than answer, she said desperately,

'I'm sorry, Jarvis, I'm afraid I have to get back.'

'Still the complete coward, I see,' he taunted. 'Are you frightened I'm going to ask other questions which you might not be able to answer either? About this man you're living with, for instance?'

Helplessly she shook her head. In the distance she thought she heard the cry of a child. Terrified that it was Sean and that he might appear at any moment, she repeated shakily, 'I have to go now—please.'

To her relief, Jarvis made no further attempt to prevent her. He merely shrugged his broad shoulders and said coldly, 'Go if you wish. I have certainly no desire to be confronted by the man you left me for, but I'll have to see you again about the divorce. Can you meet me in Port Louis, say the day after tomorrow, for lunch?'

'Yes.' She was so eager to get rid of him, she was willing to agree to almost anything.

'Whereabouts is your house?' he asked.

His pronounced lack of interest was somehow mysteriously reassuring. 'Over there,' she pointed to where it stood, at the edge of the village, praying that her apparent lack of any desire to conceal its position might alleviate any remaining curiosity.

Apparently it did, for he spared it no more than a cursory glance. His attention returning to Linsey, he stared at her intently for a long moment. Though his eyes were hooded, something flickered in the depth of them, making her start. Illogically a brief terror gripped her, but like all her impressions that morning it was fleeting and she could find nothing in Jarvis's almost casual demeanour to justify her sudden fear.

The odd flashes she imagined she was receiving were surely without substance. More probably they were a reflection of her own state of mind.

'Once you're free,' he asked sardonically, 'do you intend marrying this friend of yours?'

'No . . .'

This time the contempt he felt was clearly mirrored in the hardness of his eyes. 'Then you'd better be prepared to accept whatever I decide to settle on you,' he advised. 'When the day comes that no man wants you, you might be glad of it.'

As a red, misty anger swam before Linsey's eyes, it took all the control she had to prevent herself from telling him the truth. But for Sean's sake she had to swallow her pride and nod. 'Thank you, Jarvis,' she murmured, with an effort, 'you're very kind.'

At the note of hollow defeat in her voice, he glanced at her sharply, then he shrugged and walked away. Without another word he simply left her standing. Staring after him bleakly, Linsey wondered why the relief she expected didn't materialise. As she watched his tall figure until he was almost out of sight, she was conscious that she only felt battered and weak.

Slowly at last she wandered back to the house, her footsteps dragging, her head aching with anxiety and fear. She felt so mixed up and confused she could have burst into tears, but she knew this was a luxury she couldn't allow herself. The growing tensions of the past few weeks had had an adverse effect on Sean, making him fretful and oddly unpredictable. To see his mother upset wouldn't help at all.

Yet much as she tried to concentrate on her son, Linsey's thoughts kept returning almost feverishly to her husband. Jarvis had changed, but she would need to see more of him before she could decide exactly how much, or in what way. The shock she had experienced on first seeing him was still with her and she wished she could stop trembling, so she might be able to think clearly.

Considering everything, it was surprising that Jarvis had betrayed no great anger, or any other strong emotion, when he had found her. But if it was true what he said, that he had just been cruising by and happened to spot her, then he must have received, like herself, some kind of shock. Reluctantly she tried to gauge her own reactions in an attempt to judge his more accurately. She felt dazed, lightheaded, very shaken inside, but still slightly numb, like someone who had been stunned by a blow and hadn't yet regained complete consciousness. Bitterly she realised she needed time to pull herself together before she would be anywhere near capable of seeing anything clearly at all. It might be wasted effort, at this stage, to come to any definite conclusions.

It disturbed her, though, that Jarvis still seemed to have some kind of hold over her emotions. Since she had first met him he had had the easy ability to alter her breathing merely by looking at her. She had believed that, over the years, this peculiar kind of telepathy between them must have died. Now, apprehensively, she wasn't so sure. It wasn't until she entered the house that she managed to persuade herself that her racing pulse on the beach had been entirely due to her fear that Jarvis might find out about Sean and contrive somehow to take him away from her.

Musetta was giving Sean his breakfast when she walked into the kitchen. Sean was flushed, she could see at once that he was cross. The table was littered with crumbs which he was gathering up in handfuls and throwing at Musetta, and while Musetta protested mildly he took no notice of her. He had little respect for her as usually she allowed him to do more or less as he liked. Linsey realised that now that Harriet was gone she would have to exercise more discipline herself.

Sean was a handsome little boy and brown from being out all day in the sun. If he hadn't looked so much like Jarvis she might have passed him off as Musetta's son until Jarvis was safely away from the islands. But, as Linsey paused in the doorway, she knew this would be impossible. Anyone seeing Sean and Jarvis together would have to be very blind not to guess their exact relationship.

It hadn't been easy to let Jarvis believe she was living with another man, but now she was almost glad she had. At least it would prevent him from coming here and finding Sean. Jarvis would want to have as little to do as possible with a wife who was unfaithful to him. Yet even such a major victory left a nasty taste in her mouth, causing her to speak sharply to Sean.

Sean's mouth pursed mutinously. 'Why are you cross this morning, Mummy?' he wanted to know.

'I—I'm not cross,' she denied quickly.

'You always say I mustn't tell lies,' he frowned, 'so why do you tell them yourself?'

Linsey sighed, meeting his square on gaze with brief exasperation. Sometimes she felt Sean was older than she was. Thanks to Harriet and Musetta, he spoke both English and French fluently. This wasn't altogether surprising as both languages were used by the people of Mauritius. It was his ability to conduct a conversation in so adult a manner which caused her frequent misgivings. Somehow he never seemed to have been a child.

'I'm sorry, darling,' she made an effort to speak calmly, 'I've had rather a disturbing morning, but you know, you shouldn't throw your breakfast about.'

'I'm only naughty when I'm bored,' he answered reasonably.

'I promised to take him on the beach, Miss Linsey,' Musetta intervened with a smile. 'Now that you're back we can go now, if you like. I can tidy the house later.'

'Thank you, Musetta.' Linsey managed a weak smile, feeling grateful for anything that might divert Sean that morning. 'And don't worry about the work here. I can get on with it and—and the rest . . .'

Musetta nodded and departed with Sean in a happier mood. Linsey had decided not to tell Sean about having to leave the cottage until a later date. She and Musetta had agreed that it might be foolish to risk upsetting him before it was really necessary.

After forcing herself to drink a cup of coffee, Linsey made a belated start on sorting out Harriet's things. It wasn't easy, for although Harriet had been domineering and managing in the extreme, she had been a prop Linsey sorely missed. Sometimes she couldn't think what she was going to do without her.

As she packed the last of Harriet's clothing, she sat for a moment with her head in her hands. Harriet had been her mother's dearest friend, and a children's nannie-cum-governess to some of England's most illustrious families. When in her fifties she had gone to Mauritius to nurse her sick sister, she had decided to stay there after her sister died. Alone in the world, she had welcomed Linsey with open arms, allowing the girl to believe she was rich enough, because of what her sister had left her, to be able to support herself and half a dozen dependants, if she so wished. In fact, Linsey had earned her keep by taking over the housekeeping as Harriet's health slowly deteriorated. Nevertheless, it was Harriet who had always had the ruling say in Sean's upbringing. Occasionally Linsey had felt like rebelling against Harriet's authority, but, when it came to it, she had never been able to find the confidence to dispute her undeniable expertise.

It was very easy, now, to look back and see where she had gone wrong, but since Sean was born, or perhaps because of him, nothing had been clear-cut. If it hadn't been for Sean she would have set about finding a proper job, one which would have enabled her to be independent. As it was, she had let the weeks, the years drift by, curiously afraid of both the past and the future. Now she must be reaping the results of her continuing blindness. Harriet had died, practically penniless, not, according to her solicitor, even having owned the house she had lived in. The lease was paid up to the end of the month and Linsey had no money with which to renew it. In fiction the owner of such property often turned out to be an attractive man, who eventually married the stranded heroine, but in reality, especially in Linsey's case, the position was entirely different. The cottage belonged to a hardened business woman who was demanding vacant possession unless a whole year's rent was paid in advance.

CHAPTER TWO

LINSEY slept in a narrow single bed in a room scarcely large enough to hold it. The cottage had three bedrooms, but only the one which had been Harriet's was of any size. Linsey could have taken it over, but was reluctant to do so. Apart from anything else it didn't seem worth it for so short a time.

She had gone to bed early because she felt tired, but she was finding it impossible to sleep. In the end she stopped trying and attempted to work out some sort of plan for the future. Yet Jarvis kept coming between her and everything else. Impatiently she tossed and turned, clenching her hands. With so many immediate problems demanding her complete concentration, it vexed her that she could only think of him. And while this was probably only to be expected, after meeting him again after being apart for so long, it disturbed her greatly that he appeared to be dominating her thoughts.

Falling at last into an uneasy sleep, she woke with a start, convinced that someone was standing outside her window. Sitting up with a curling sensation of fright, she stared at the uncurtained glass, relieved to find no one there. Feeling oddly breathless, she sank back against her pillows, her eyes glued to the moonwashed panes. Moonlight lit the room to a daytime brilliance, but would only have revealed her sleeping quietly. Harriet had never been one for gathering costly possessions, there was nothing here to attract a thief. Sean slept in his cot next door with Musetta to keep an eye on him. Harriet had decided this would be the best arrangement, after he was born and Linsey had still been far from well.

Pulling herself together, Linsey went quietly to see that Sean and Musetta were all right. Musetta's dark curly head lay undisturbed on her pillow while Sean slept soundly. There was no other sound but the occasional snuffle of his breathing and, reassured, Linsey returned to her own room.

This incident, which she decided must have been part of a bad dream, didn't help her to get back to sleep. Again her thoughts turned to Jarvis, to the first time she had met him. Linsey's father, a man in his early forties, had joined Jarvis's firm within a year of leaving university, but it wasn't until just before he died that he had achieved top management level. One evening, coming home from work, he had been knocked down by a careless driver in the firm's car park. He had been taken to hospital where he had to stay for several days. Jarvis, by some coincidence, had been with him at the time, and afterwards he had gone to Peter Brown's house to break the news to his wife.

Linsey's mother had answered the door and, after Jarvis said he would like to speak to her, had asked him to come in. Linsey had been in the lounge playing records and turned to glance curiously at Jarvis. She had felt slightly stunned by the impact of his hard good looks and bewildered by the way her stomach was behaving as she met the narrowed intentness of his eyes. She hadn't been able to decide if it was Jarvis or the fright she had received on hearing about her father's accident that had made her tremble so.

After those first few seconds, Jarvis Parradine hadn't seemed to take any more notice of the slender young girl whose beauty, by any standards, was remarkable. He had been kind, Linsey remembered. He had taken her mother to the hospital to visit her father. Linsey had gone, too, and he had insisted on driving them both home again. He said very little to Linsey, but she had been very conscious of something almost tangible between them, drawing them together. Somehow, she hadn't been at all surprised when a few days later he rang and asked her to have dinner with him.

Linsey had accepted while her voice and hands shook. Selfconsciously she had sensed that he was aware of her nervousness, for there seemed to be a hint of amusement in his voice as he had arranged to pick her up. She hadn't told her parents where she was going as she had been wary of the speculation this might cause, and she couldn't imagine Jarvis asking her out more than once. While she might be pretty and fairly intelligent, when it came down to it, what could she and a man like Jarvis Parradine have in common? He might appreciate a pretty face, but she was sure he would hate being bored.

Having arranged to be ready by seven-thirty, she didn't expect him to arrive almost half an hour earlier, just as she was stepping out of her bath. When her father, now home and fully recovered, had gone to the door, he had been astonished to find Jarvis standing on the door-step.

Wryly Linsey recalled how her parents had been quite dazed to think that Jarvis should be interested in their daughter. Their bewilderment, after he had taken her out several times, had subsided, after which they had both reacted in different ways. Mrs Brown was naturally excited that Jarvis Parradine had apparently taken a fancy to her daughter, while Peter Brown was inclined to be more cautious.

'I shouldn't take him too seriously, if I were you,' he advised his starry-eyed daughter. 'He's a brilliant man, but older than you—he must be at least thirty-three or four. And he's been around, you know.'

Linsey, however, was not prepared to listen to something she had no wish to hear. She was eighteen, had left school and had already decided to make a career of nursing. After her training she needn't necessarily stay in the same hospital. She could travel, get work like Harriet, her mother's friend, in any part of the world. Of course she hadn't allowed for meeting someone like Jarvis, but the decisions she had already made, regarding her future, convinced her she was entirely grown up and well able to deal with a man like him.

She often wondered why he had only kissed her once between meeting her and marrying her. After that one occasion her mouth had been so bruised, she had innocently assured herself that she was glad he made no attempt to repeat the performance. All the same, she had felt a little bewildered and disappointed when he had contented himself with merely kissing her lightly on the cheek afterwards. Not until their wedding night, when she had had a rather rude awakening, had she wished she was back on that almost platonic footing.

They had dined in his wonderful old house in the country. He had another house in London, but he considered Worton Manor his real home. His mother was still alive, but as she was living in Paris at the time, Linsey didn't meet her. It had been summer, a warm, balmy night, and later, when it was almost dark and the servants retired, Jarvis had taken her in his arms.

In her narrow bed, Linsey swallowed, startled by the tremors which unmercifully shook her body as the memory of that moment came rushing back. Within the tightening circle of his arms she had stood quite still, too shy and confused to do anything else. When she didn't struggle he pulled her closer, one arm and hand holding her to him while, with the other, he gently drew the confining pins from her hair.

When it had fallen in a fair, shining cascade down her shoulders, he had drawn a deep breath of satisfaction. 'It's far too lovely to be imprisoned,' he smiled, nothing in his eyes to suggest he was about to kiss her ruthlessly.

Linsey had scarcely dared raise her own eyes to look at him, afraid of what he might read in them, but she had been somewhat reassured by his teasing tones. After a minute, although her heart was beating jerkily, she managed to ask carelessly, 'Don't you like a girl to look tidy?'

'Sometimes,' he agreed sardonically. 'Just as long as she doesn't mind being made untidy, occasionally.'

'Oh!' Because she wasn't sure of his meaning, the colour in her cheeks had fluctuated enchantingly. She sensed, though, that it might be enough to make her blush even more deeply than she was doing now.

Remorselessly, he had gone on, his voice light but his eyes glinting, 'I'd like to see you in my bed, with your hair all mussed up and tangled about us.'

'Oh!' Linsey had said again, but this time her breathless exclamation had contained shock. Jarvis had never talked to her like this before and she wasn't sure that she liked it. Worse than that, for all he sounded so cool he might easily just be teasing her, it could mean he was used to the kind of women who wouldn't think twice about letting him make love to them. More than once since they had met, hadn't he hinted, with a faintly jibing note in his voice, at her innocence, yet she had never pretended to be anything else. But on the whole, apart from odd moments like this, he had been an attentive and very properly behaved escort.

Even now, he regarded her so whimsically she found it difficult to take exception to what he was saying, but as the silence between them lengthened and his face grew curiously taut, she felt she ought to make some kind of a stand. If Jarvis was seriously attempting to discover if she'd be willing to sleep with him, there could be no better time to straighten him out.

Trying not to look too shaken and depressed, she began pushing away from him. 'I think I'd better go home now, Jarvis, if you don't mind.'

'At least you have that little line off pat,' he mocked derisively.

'Well then?' she had paused, her hands locked against his chest, glancing up at him, her eyes deliberately cool.

Her apparent coolness triggered something off. In the following moment, when it seemed he would let her go, he changed his mind.

'Not yet,' he muttered thickly, his mouth swooping down to catch hers unawares.

Linsey had been kissed before and she didn't suspect, although he excited her, that Jarvis's kisses were going to be any different from the others she had known. How mistaken she was, he proved in that first brief encounter. Fire seemed to flash between them, making her wince. She flinched away from him in blind panic, unconsciously raising her hands to claw at his face.

As their lips met she heard his smothered gasp, even as he caught her hysterical hands, pinning them behind her back. With his swift strength he immobilised her so completely she couldn't move. And, as if to punish her for his scratched face, his mouth continued to crush hers while his free hand ran carelessly over the palpitating rise and fall of her breast.

She thought, her mind hazy and frightened, that eventually, when he stopped treating her so roughly, he might throw her out. A kind of violence seemed to move in him. She had hurt him and he was clearly angry. It must be her fright and his anger combining to make her feel she was swiftly losing her wits.

Suddenly he lifted his head and stared at her, deliberately seeking and holding her gaze. As her glance helplessly met his, she saw flames flaring deep in the depth of his eyes. She had thought he would thrust her away, but instead, with a sigh, he lowered his mouth to hers again, as if she was a temptation he couldn't resist.

His mouth began making urgent movements against her own, prizing her lips apart, while his hands gripped

with renewed intensity. Her own hands, freed, somehow found their way around his neck, as she battled
helplessly against the increasing surge of his passion.
If she had been convinced that the feeling between
them couldn't be ignited twice, she was proved wrong.
Another moment she was floating, unaware of her surroundings, conscious only of Jarvis's probing lips and
of the flames searing her through them.

Then he had stopped kissing her and drawn back,
this time quite sharply. In a terse voice he had asked,
'How do you feel? Are you frightened?'

She had thought it a strange question. Was she
frightened? she wondered, confused. She supposed she
was, but she knew she was also excited. It was a new
sensation, and she stared back at him with both eager-
ness and terror in her eyes. 'A little,' she confessed.

His eyes were half closed and curiously glittering. 'I
am,' he jeered, his voice extremely dry, as if he didn't
quite believe it. 'What is there about you, Linsey
Brown, to make me feel this way?'

Feeling mortally offended, she had pulled away from
him and he had taken her home without another word.
It had been a month before she had heard from him
again, four whole weeks during which she had been
unable to think of anything or anyone else. Then he
rang and said he had arranged for them to be married.
He hadn't asked if she would marry him. He had apparently taken it for granted that she would, and, while
she hated him for what she termed his arrogant high-
handedness, she had found herself meekly agreeing
with every plan he had made.

As Linsey's thoughts would have travelled on towards her wedding day, she refused to go with them.
Dawn was breaking and, suffocated by the smallness
of her bedroom and by memories which had not been
allowed to surface for years, she tumbled out of bed.
Without waiting to as much as don her light wrapper,

she fled from the house, down to the beach.

There was no one about, and as the house was a little way from the village, there was nothing between it and the sea. As the sun wasn't yet up the sand was still lovely and cool beneath her feet as she ran swiftly towards the water. Once there, as she had done hundreds of times before, she stepped quickly out of her brief nightdress and plunged into the waves.

She swam out a long way, trying to purge her mind of all further thought of Jarvis, little realising he was again standing on the deck of his yacht watching her. She didn't know that again he had paced the decks since first light, his binoculars already in his hands. She never suspected he had them trained on the house as she ran out of it, or that he had watched the swift disposal of her silky night attire with hard, expressionless eyes. It was only as he viewed her naked figure before it disappeared under the waves that his mouth curled in cruel anticipation.

Linsey swam and dived like a dolphin, unaware that she had an audience. If she had noticed the yacht far out in the bay, she wouldn't have believed anyone on board would have bothered to give her more than a brief glance, if they had been looking her way. Boats came and went, but most of them anchored for the night closer inshore, in one of the many little bays, or in the capital, Port Louis. No one, during all the years she had been here, had ever violated their privacy. The villagers, kindly, courteous people, might have known how she liked to swim in the early mornings, but never came near. They liked the English girl and never once had she done anything to lose the affection and regard they had for her. They had, in fact, developed an almost protective attitude towards Linsey and her small son. From Miss Harriet they had learned discreetly that Linsey's husband had turned out to be no good, and, although Linsey herself never mentioned him, they felt sorry that such a lovely young girl should have been left to bring up her son on her own.

During the following night, Linsey had another bad dream. Again she woke with a frightened start to feel that someone was standing outside her window. And, as on the previous night, she found it difficult to convince herself there was no one there. The next morning, still doubtful, she even went to the back of the house to look for footprints. She didn't find any, as the green lawn which Harriet had loved and cultivated so assiduously swept right up under the windows. Linsey couldn't find so much as one mark marring its smooth perfection. With a sigh of half impatient frustration, she went to have her swim before trying to arrange the daily chores so that she wouldn't be late for her meeting with Jarvis in Port Louis.

Sean wanted to go, too. 'You never take me anywhere,' he complained, his small face sullen as he watched his mother applying a light make-up to her face. She had remembered how Jarvis had liked her to look well groomed when he took her out and she thought, considering everything, it might be wiser to try and please him.

It seemed her young son would also have to be appeased. Ruefully she laid down her pink lipstick. 'You know I haven't been able to go far lately, because of Harriet.'

'But she died—and I like Port Louis,' he said quickly. 'There's a lot going on there.'

Linsey put out a hand to straighten his dark, unruly hair. 'I'm sure you'll be much happier on the beach,' she replied gently but firmly. 'And I won't be away long. Tomorrow,' she promised rashly, 'I'll take you anywhere you like.'

'I get tired of being with women,' he retorted coldly, pushing her hand away.

Startled, Linsey frowned. Sean was continually surprising her, but it was the first time he had come out with anything like this. She was soon to be enlightened.

'Musetta says I should have other boys to talk to.'

So it was something Musetta had been saying? She might have known. Yet Musetta would have meant no harm. It wasn't her fault that Sean must interpret almost everything with a wisdom far beyond his actual years.

Linsey tried to smile. 'Well, you do play with Jules and Brian occasionally, and the boys in the village.' Jules and Brian lived on a nearby sugar plantation. Harriet had been friendly with their grandmother and Jules and Brian were the sons of one of Mrs Lanier's two sons.

'Yeah, I know,' Sean shrugged his small shoulders irritably, 'but they've got a proper home, and proper parents.'

Linsey worried over this as she waited in the village for the bus which would take her to Port Louis. Sean could be hurtful—just like his father. Then, annoyed with herself, she admitted it was no use thinking this way about a little boy of three. All families had their difficulties, whether they were one-parent ones or not. Having two parents didn't automatically turn children into angels. At least Sean didn't have to endure the tensions which could arise when parents lived together but didn't get on with each other.

Thus, Linsey argued with herself as she waited, feeling tensely at odds with the drowsy beauty of the morning. Sean might think life was dull, but he would do better with her, away from his father's inborn arrogance, of which he already seemed to have inherited too much. All she had to do at the moment was to concentrate on keeping the two of them apart. But, as she assured herself constantly, if by some chance Jarvis did find out about Sean, there was nothing he could do about it. It was merely the discomfort of such a meeting that she was determined to avoid.

When a car drew up beside her, she was so immersed in her thoughts that she jumped. Her eyes widened, then sharpened with fright when she saw it was Jarvis. Why was he here? Had he come to spy on her? Her tightening nerves seemed to be laughing at her newly found self-confidence as she stared at him in dismay.

As if the apprehension on her face convinced him she was ready to run at any moment, he was out of the car in a flash, with his hand on her arm.

'Good morning, Linsey,' he greeted her coolly, while his touch burned her flesh. 'I forgot to arrange where to meet you, so I thought I'd better come here. There was a hold-up on the road or I should have been here sooner and saved you the trouble of having to walk to the bus stop.' He frowned down on her, obviously under the impression that the heat in her cheeks was due to exertion. 'Wouldn't it have been easier to have taken a taxi?'

It was simpler to shake her head and allow him to help her politely into the front seat of his hired car. 'I realised we'd made no definite arrangements, but I was going to the harbour. I expected to find you there.'

He shot her a quick glance out of the corner of his eyes as he got in beside her and turned the car in the direction of Port Louis. 'But it wasn't something that worried you greatly, whether you found me or not, I mean?'

Unconsciously she rubbed the arm he had gripped so tightly, wishing it would stop tingling. 'You're mistaken,' she replied, quite truthfully, knowing that if she hadn't found him he would probably have come looking for her at the house, and that was the last thing she would have wanted. Her throat thick, she swallowed. 'I'd like to have everything settled as much as you.'

To her dismay, instead of discussing this, he began talking idly about the island. 'You must have led an idyllic kind of life here, with your boy-friends? Or has it only been one? The same one?'

Uncomfortably, she kept her eyes on the road. 'Yes,' she murmured.

'How interesting,' he observed smoothly, eyes flicking her tense figure. 'Somehow I never think of you as being the faithful type.'

Much as Linsey tried to suppress a retort, she was unable to find the control. 'You have a nerve!' she burst out. 'When I think of your girl-friends . . .'

'Ah, but I didn't leave you for one of them,' he pointed out blandly. 'It was you who went the whole hog. Is he a sugar planter, who perhaps met you in London and managed to entice you here, or is he English, like yourself?'

'Like me,' she whispered nervously, not knowing what else to say.

'You aren't very forthcoming, are you?' he mocked. 'Tell me, are you very much in love with him?'

'What has all this to do with our divorce?' she cried hoarsely. 'My private life is none of your business.'

'You think not?' His voice was suddenly icy. 'You'd be surprised.'

Immediately she thought she understood. 'You're trying to trick me so you won't have to pay me anything! Well . . .'

'No such thing,' he cut in, before she could protest that she didn't want any of his money. 'Do you really believe I would miss anything I'd have to pay you? I wasn't even thinking of money.'

Doubtfully, Linsey glanced at him, shocked to find her eyes clinging to his strong, decisive profile as if trying to memorise every little detail of Jarvis's dark, handsome face against another stretch of lonely years when she would have no hope of ever seeing him again. Because she had to fight an overwhelming impulse to touch him, she found herself retorting, almost defiantly, 'If it has nothing to do with alimony, then you must be trying to discover someone whom you can name as co-respondent.'

'Not particularly,' his mouth twisted cynically. 'My pride won't suffer half as much if we leave it as desertion. I have no particular wish to know your lover's name or any other such details. Always supposing you could supply them, of course.'

What did he mean by that? Startled, Linsey bit her lip. Had it merely been a slip of the tongue? Had he not meant to say 'would' instead of 'could'? Surely this was it? She had never given Jarvis any reason to doubt her story. Uneasily she lapsed into silence, thinking this was safer, but her eyes were filled with an unaccountable apprehension as they rested on his tightening hands on the wheel.

The road ran among sun-drenched sugar-cane fields and palm trees. On one side was the sea, while on the other were vast plains of sugar-cane and dramatic volcanic peaks and mountains. In the rivers which they passed, sari-clad women were occasionally to be seen, washing clothes, and the sleepy little fishing villages with their neat little houses and shacks provided yet another contrast to some of the massive old colonial mansions which dotted the countryside. Mauritius wasn't a large island, it was only about forty miles long by thirty miles wide, but in both people and scenery it offered endless variety.

Usually Linsey loved it, but today she felt unable to relax. When at last they drove into Port Louis she could have cried with relief. Fervently she hoped that by the time they found some place to eat, Jarvis might have lost interest in her affairs. Otherwise she was going to find it difficult to parry his peculiarly devious questions.

Glancing around, she was surprised to find he was making for the harbour, and while she had been initially going to search for him there, surely it wasn't necessary to go there now?

'Where are you taking me?' she asked quickly, trying

to hide her alarm. He had mentioned his yacht but said nothing about having lunch on it.

Apparently this was his intention. 'You'll like it,' he assured her coolly. 'Every woman I've had on board yet has been in raptures over it, and a lot of them would be much more sophisticated than you are.'

While Linsey could believe this, it didn't make her feel any better. Nervously she glanced at him. 'Please, Jarvis, couldn't we go somewhere else? Somewhere where you aren't known?'

He smiled at her odd request as he parked the car. 'Are you worried about how I'm going to introduce you?'

'It could be embarrassing.' A fine colour crept under the porcelain texture of her skin and her blue eyes widened appealingly.

Grimly he ignored her plea. 'Not, I'm sure, as embarrassing as it was for me, having to explain your sudden absence to my friends. If you remember, we were giving a dinner party that evening. It had to be cancelled, of course, and some of the guests, I suspect, still harbour suspicions that I secretly did away with you.'

After the first flicker of anger, which she wondered if she had imagined, he spoke so dryly she wasn't sure if he was serious or joking. Again she flushed. 'I didn't forget about the party, Jarvis. I just didn't know what to do about it . . .'

'So in the end you decided to do nothing, for all you knew that some of the people who were coming were very important.'

'I'm sorry,' she apologised helplessly, hating him for reminding her of it, but feeling terribly at fault. Suddenly she knew he was still angry about the dinner party—and a lot of other things he wasn't letting on about at the moment. Fright overwhelming her, she turned quickly to leave him, but he caught hold of her firmly.

'You aren't running away this time, Linsey.'

'I was ill, the first time,' she muttered, thinking how

easily he had forgotten.

'Not too ill to get yourself on a plane and come here,' he jeered harshly.

'I was worse when I arrived,' she said tonelessly, not wanting to recall the weeks of misery that had followed. 'As for your guests, I'm sure you managed to explain away my absence very convincingly.'

She didn't like the angle of his jaw as he whipped from the car, but when he reached her side of it he was smiling. Deliberately, she felt, so as not to antagonise her any further, but, because of Sean, she managed to restrain the flurry of even sharper words that trembled on the tip of her tongue.

Obediently she got out beside him as, with a movement that confirmed her suspicions regarding his sudden tolerance, Jarvis wrenched open her door. She remained silent, however, waiting quietly while he locked the car up. Nor did she protest again about lunching on his yacht, but she did feel like screaming when he renewed his hold on her arm, running mocking fingers swiftly down it to grip her wrist. That her pulse was beating twice as fast as it did normally she tried to deny by inserting some extra coolness into her voice.

'Does your crew know you're married?' she asked. She hadn't seen his yacht, so she couldn't be sure he had a crew, but unless it was very small she doubted that he would be sailing it himself. The kind of craft he had hinted at suggested opulence rather than a lack of size.

'Yes,' his face went cold again, 'they know I'm a married man, that's something I've never tried to hide. They didn't know, though, that my wife was living here until I mentioned it this morning, and you may be sure they're all eager to meet you.'

Curious, more likely. Linsey flushed, holding back. 'I still wish you would change your mind and have lunch in the town, Jarvis.'

'And I'd like you to please me for once,' he said, his tone so inflexible, she wasn't sure if she had a choice. 'You don't think I'm going to kidnap you, do you?'

Linsey's flush faded to leave her stark white and very frightened. This hadn't occurred to her. It did now, and shock went lancing through her. 'Oh, no,' she whispered, 'not that!'

Jarvis stared at her pale face narrowly. 'Would it matter if I did?' he taunted. 'With your mother's well-meaning friend dead, who's to miss you? Apart from a servant, perhaps, if you have one.'

She was too panic-stricken to realise he made no mention of the man she was supposed to be living with. Her mind was too busy searching for reasons as to why it was imperative that she return to the house immediately after lunch. 'Musetta is something more than just a servant,' she said. 'She's not very old, but she was with Harriet for years, long before I came, and she's grown fond of me. If I disappeared she would go to the police, and they don't take kindly to—to kidnapping.'

'Don't they?' his brows rose indifferently. 'I think you're barking up the wrong tree. As you're my wife they might think twice before they intervened. People on these islands still believe that families should stay together.'

Linsey had an awful feeling he could be right. Then, fortunately, her confused thoughts settled on something else. 'But there wouldn't be much point in carrying me off, would there? I mean——' she tried to smile lightly, 'you want a divorce. You wouldn't want my company when you're doing your best to get rid of me?'

'Quite right,' he replied smoothly, 'so you can calm yourself, my dear. You're jumping to all the wrong conclusions, while I have no intention of keeping you from your lover any longer than necessary. You must learn not to take everything I say quite so seriously.'

So he hadn't forgotten her non-existent lover. She should have remembered he never forgot a thing. Silently she hated him for his mocking smile and for putting her in such an awkward position. He might have no intention of taking her anywhere against her will, but he did intend parading her before the curious eyes of the men he employed on his boat. Knowing how much she would hate this, he had deliberately taken this opportunity of humiliating her.

A mass of ragged nerves churning inside her, Linsey made no reply to his last comment but walked seething by his side. From Harbour Square they quickly reached the docks where his yacht was moored. Jarvis, after a briefly cynical glance at her set face, was silent himself, concentrating on steering her safely through the crowds on the quayside.

His yacht was superb, but Linsey was still so agitated she scarcely noticed. Fortunately, because of this, she was barely conscious of the interested surveillance of Jarvis's crew, as she went on board. It wasn't until minutes later, in the saloon, that the opulence around her really began to register.

Slightly dazed, she allowed her eyes to wander. The yacht must have cost a fortune to fit out, let alone buy. Now she thought she understood why Jarvis had brought her here. It had nothing to do with the crew; it was so she could understand something of what she had given up when she had left him. Jarvis had a lot of pride and he wasn't wholly English. He was related to some of Europe's most distinguished families, and it probably wasn't his fault that pride seemed, sometimes, as if it might have been bred in his very bones. Linsey had occasionally wondered, during the first weeks of their marriage, exactly what kind of blood he had in his veins. If it was responsible for the trace of hard ruthlessness in his character, the touch of unforgiving arrogance he had frequently displayed.

It was this that made her shiver now, despite the warmth of the day. She felt almost grateful when he interrupted her uneasy thoughts by telling her to sit down. It was an order, not a request, but on obeying him blindly, she was surprised when he asked, in quite a friendly voice, if she was comfortable.

'Yes, thank you,' she said.

Listening to her stiff little reply, he smiled slightly and went to pour her a drink.

'Why not try to relax?' he suggested soothingly, placing a dry sherry in her unsteady hands.

'How can I?' Linsey unconsciously tightened her fingers around the stem of her glass, while her eyes, without her knowing it, widened with mute appeal on his. 'We have to talk about the divorce. We can't put off talking about it for ever.'

His eyes were curiously veiled. 'I only picked you up not much more than an hour ago.'

'But this wasn't intended as a social visit, was it?' she protested unevenly.

Laconically, his strongly shaped mouth twisted. 'We have plenty of time to discuss—anything you like, but there's no hurry. I suggest we eat first and talk later. The chef has prepared something extra delicious in your honour, I believe, so why risk ruining our appetites?'

CHAPTER THREE

JARVIS'S attitude bewildered Linsey. He sounded so reasonable she could do nothing else but agree with him. Reluctantly she nodded, while trying to dismiss her continuing conviction that everything was not quite as it should be. Feeling badly in need of it, she stared down into the golden depth of her drink, yet could scarcely bring herself to drink it.

As Jarvis turned to get something for himself, her glance followed him apprehensively. He was casually dressed in a light shirt and tight but well-fitting pants which seemed to reveal every muscle of his tall, powerful figure. There was enough sheer masculinity about him to make any woman's pulse beat faster, and Linsey felt something inside her responding as it had always done.

Despairingly she winced, wondering how he could still make her feel this way after so long. It must have something to do with the fact that she had been his wife, and old feelings were difficult to eliminate altogether. She hadn't thought she would remember what it was like to lie in his arms, and when she recalled the ruthless hardness of his body, taut with urgency against her own, she shivered.

Jarvis had been too experienced a lover to leave any room for criticism on that score. It must have been her own total lack of experience that had prevented her from enjoying what he had offered as much as she might have done. Her heart beating loudly, she wondered if she would be so reticent now. Somehow she doubted it. She was too aware of a sensuous kind of hunger building up inside her to try and deny it.

And it was a feeling which frightened her, for she didn't know how long she could control it.

Heat coloured Linsey's skin as she suddenly realised the direction her thoughts had taken. Hastily dragging her eyes from Jarvis's broad back, she took a quick gulp of her sherry.

She was still flushed when he returned, drink in hand, to sit beside her, and she knew he was curious, because his eyes grew intent on her hot cheeks. 'My crew are quite impressed, or didn't you notice?'

She wished he had sat farther away. This near she could see too much of him. He had undone the top buttons of his shirt, revealing the crisply curling dark hair on his chest. Something else she didn't want to remember!

'Impressed . . . With what?' she asked stupidly.

'With you, of course,' he returned thinly, as if something suddenly displeased him. 'It amazes me how taken in men can be by a pretty face, even allowing for the fact that yours is above average.'

Tightly, she retorted, 'And that's all you consider me to be—a pretty face?'

'Is it my fault,' he drawled cruelly, 'that I was scarcely allowed more than a glimpse of what lay behind it?'

'But you're convinced there's nothing much?'

'My dear girl,' he rejoined coolly, 'during the brief spell of our honeymoon I'm afraid it wasn't your mind I was concentrating on. Afterwards, after you ran away from me, I began to believe there might be something wrong with it, but your flight here and your apparent ability to forget your responsibilities and enjoy the fleshpots of life assures me I was greatly mistaken.'

Unhappily, Linsey bit her lip at such castigation. Anger flared inside her, yet how could she defend herself without betraying her secret? Hanging desperately on to the tattered remnants of her composure, she muttered feebly, 'We didn't have much time to get to know each other, what with my parents and—and everything.'

Jarvis appeared about to reply sharply, then changed his mind. 'We seem to be back at square one,' he snapped contemptuously, 'and, as I said before, why spoil a pleasant day?'

Linsey felt oddly frightened by this, although she told herself sternly it was foolish to read sinister meanings in everything he said. Trying not to sound nervous, she murmured haltingly, 'You only mentioned lunch.'

The impatient breath he drew spoke volumes. 'What if I did?' he rapped. 'Before we finish here and I get you home, the best part of the day will be gone.'

'Of course,' she replied, feeling utterly naïve, while wondering if she would ever survive so long, with all the tension between them. By the minute she could feel it developing. She had been conscious of it to a certain extent when they had met on the beach that first morning. Then, on her part, she had decided it had arisen from fright. Now she wasn't so sure any more where it was coming from, but each time their eyes met it seemed as though invisible threads were pulling them together.

She was aware, now, of Jarvis's close regard but kept her own eyes fixed on her drink. Presently, when they went to the dining-room, she fancied he was still watching her grimly and did her best to walk steadily, although her legs felt quite shaky. She wore a white, sleeveless dress which she had made herself and while she knew she looked very nice in it, with her slender figure and fair, silky hair, she didn't feel she was beautiful enough to warrant the protracted attention of a man as used to lovely women as her husband.

Waving his servants aside, Jarvis saw her seated himself, and, to her utter astonishment, after pushing her chair in, he let his hands linger gently on her shoulders. 'All right?' he asked smoothly.

With a mute nod, Linsey waited tensely for him to take his hands away and was relieved when he did so immediately. He seemed far too concerned for her comfort all of a sudden and again she was swamped by elusive suspicions. Why should he be trying to give his men the impression that his wife mattered to him when they must know they hadn't lived together for years?

Jarvis sat down opposite her and after seeing she had enough to eat and drink began talking to her about the islands. Linsey, pushing her food around on her plate, answered in monosyllables. Her appetite had deserted her, she would as soon have had a sandwich and a glass of lemonade on deck. She wasn't used to being waited on hand and foot by uniformed stewards, who divided their time between studying her and serving the food. She met the quick admiration in their eyes as coolly as she could without seeming aloof, and wasn't aware that she said please and thank you with the politeness of a nicely brought up child. She didn't know that when viewing her curiously innocent young face, they found it difficult to believe she was married, and especially to a man like Jarvis Parradine.

The meal, though beautifully cooked and served, seemed to drag endlessly. Linsey felt almost weak with relief when it was over and they were back in the saloon again. She wasn't ready yet to admit that Jarvis's close proximity was affecting her more than she would ever have thought it could. She had imagined herself quite safe from his undeniable charm, convinced that the years must have built within her some kind of immunity. Now, while he angered her frequently by some of the taunting remarks he made, she realised uneasily that anger might not be the strongest feeling she would find if she were to take a long, hard look at her emotions.

Surely, she prayed desperately, accepting the delicious black coffee which was offered her, there could be nothing left of the attraction they had once felt for each other. Urgently she found herself searching for reasons why she shouldn't care for him any more. Glancing at him carefully, as he broodingly surveyed the glass of brandy he was turning slowly in his hands, she saw more clearly than she had done before that he had aged. There was silver among the dark hair at his temples and the lines around his eyes seemed even more deeply etched than they had on the beach, as if he wasn't sleeping well. Or perhaps he wasn't sleeping alone. Remembering how demanding he could be, Linsey flushed. As a lover, he often hadn't believed in sleeping much at all.

For all she was convinced she would never want him back as her lover again, the thought of him with other women made her feel sick. He was no monk, but after they were married he had devoted himself to his wife entirely. Even after their honeymoon, when they had become more or less strangers to each other, she had never suspected him of being unfaithful, not until she had found him in his office with Olivia James.

Since she had left him, of course, it would be unnatural for a man like him if he hadn't sought consolation elsewhere. So why did she find herself hoping fervently that if there was someone else she would never have to meet her? Maybe it was still Olivia? Perhaps that was why he wanted a divorce, so he would be free to marry her.

'A penny for them?'

Jarvis's dry voice cutting through her thoughts made Linsey start. She had forgotten she was staring at him and now she was terrified he had read what was on her mind. Jarvis had once been very good at this, where she was concerned.

To her dismay, instead of parrying his query with a

cool little smile, she found herself babbling in confusion, 'I was thinking about the yacht. It seems large for just one man.'

'Don't you mean extravagant?'

She shook her head. 'Does it really belong to you, or do you just charter it?'

'It belongs to me,' he said pleasantly. 'I use it for both business and pleasure. In between times I hire it out to friends, so it practically pays for itself.'

'Does it have to?'

'No.'

Just that. Linsey could have wished, somehow, that his answer had been different. For Sean's sake, as well as her own, she might have felt better if Jarvis had confessed himself short of money. Immediately she flushed, imagining he might believe she was trying to probe about his financial affairs. This wasn't the case, though, as she discovered when he spoke again.

'Did you imagine I used it for entertaining other women?'

If she owned to thinking this he might easily conclude she was jealous, yet how could she deny what might be plainly written on her face? 'I—I did wonder . . .' Why, after all, should she be untruthful over this? She was only surprised by the sudden pain that lanced through her as he nodded his head.

'Sometimes I do, but they're mostly the wives of business associates who accompany their husbands. Not every man,' he added, with a brutal frankness, 'has an insatiable desire for sex.'

'But you enjoyed it, once,' she stammered, her cheeks hot, amazed that she could be so outspoken.

'Is that another way of calling me a liar?' he drawled. 'What we had, Linsey, wasn't always so enjoyable. You were very young, a virgin when I married you, and if I didn't keep that in mind, you complained.'

'Sometimes——' she hesitated, perspiration beading

her brow, for she had never had a conversation like this in her life. Licking dried lips, she tried again. 'Sometimes you were too—too . . .'

'Demanding?' he cut in. 'You couldn't cope with me, you mean? God in heaven, Linsey!' he snarled, 'didn't you ever guess what you did to a man? Didn't you realise I didn't treat you half as roughly as I might have done? You cried off, then ran after me later, expecting me, I suppose, to go down on my knees and grovel. It wasn't as if you weren't capable of meeting me more than halfway, either. All you had to do was get rid of a few inhibitions, and the prim little image you had of yourself.'

Aghast, Linsey stared at him, meeting his cold anger with wide, disturbed eyes. So that was what he had thought? She knew there was more than a grain of truth in his accusations. On her wedding night—no, she wouldn't think of that, but, later, she had been alarmed by what seemed the increasing wildness of her own passion. Often she hadn't dared let go, for fear of what Jarvis might think. Now, when she saw with utter confusion where her selfconsciousness had led to, she felt more bewildered and hurt than ever.

Helplessly, her cheeks burning scarlet, she shook her head, as if to get rid of the doubts that tormented her. She was here to discuss a divorce, wasn't she? Not to dwell on past mistakes, or what might have been.

'Jarvis?' she began, then suddenly, to her horror, she realised the boat was moving. Jumping to her feet, she rushed to the window. Sure enough, they were leaving the harbour, sailing past the part where some deep-sea vessels were moored to buoys in the roadstead. 'We can't be!' she exclaimed, her voice rising apprehensively. 'Jarvis . . .'

As she turned back to him, she saw he was watching her carefully, his eyes glittering with hard calculation—

an expression so swiftly replaced by a silky indifference that she blanched.

'Yes?' he prompted, as she grabbed his arm hysterically. 'What is it?'

'You know very well what it is!' she gasped indignantly, almost in tears with rage and fright. 'The boat's sailing!'

'Ah, yes,' he said, 'so it is.'

She gritted clenched teeth. 'But where are we going?'

'I didn't have anywhere particular in mind,' he shrugged. 'We can just cruise around, if you like.'

'You . . .' She tried to control herself, for it might not be as bad as it looked and she had no wish to make a fool of herself. Letting go of his arm she asked, 'You mean, only for an hour or two?'

He smiled mockingly. 'Or a day or two. Even a few days. I'm sure you'll enjoy sailing with me.'

'If you're serious, you must be crazy!'

'I was once, over you.'

'But not now?' Caught on the raw, she stared at him, everything else momentarily, mysteriously forgotten.

'No, my dear Linsey,' he replied suavely, 'that's scarcely how I'd describe my feelings after all this time. Four years changes a man.'

'Then,' she whispered tersely, 'you wouldn't find my company entertaining, so why try and keep me here against my will?'

'There are different kinds of entertainment,' he paused, and his reflective smile frightened her. 'At least I shouldn't be bored.'

Linsey could feel her heart fluttering in her breast like a panic-stricken sparrow she had once rescued from a big cat. Why didn't someone come and save her? Of course there was no one. She was all alone in the world apart from Sean, and he wasn't old enough to even look after himself.

'I have to go home!' she blazed up at Jarvis fiercely. 'Kindly order your men to turn back at once!'

'I don't make a habit of giving new orders every five minutes when I'm at sea. Not unnaturally, it leads to confusion.' His eyes lingered closely on the agitated rise and fall of her breast, as though he was measuring her panic in heartbeats. 'Surely this lover of yours won't miss you all that much?'

'He will! And—and I should miss him desperately.' It was imperative that she make Jarvis regret what he was doing, but she had never been good at pretence. He wasn't easy to fool. His dark eyes seemed to be studying her every movement, making her falter.

'How interesting,' he murmured, his eyes raking her intense face with contemptuous amusement. 'What if I were to make sure you don't?'

At the mocking taunt in Jarvis's voice, Linsey's panic turned into frenzy. She began hitting him, her small, fragile fists ineffectual at first but gathering strength with momentum, and the force of her feelings. 'I hate you, I hate you!' she cried, believing she meant it.

'You little wildcat!' He put up with her frantic attack for only so long before catching hold of her flying fists and rendering her helpless. As her breath caught on an apprehensive sob, he dragged her savagely to him. 'I should have tamed you long ago,' he snarled, 'I should have subdued you by methods that might have turned you into an obedient wife, instead of leaving you alone to get over the baby.'

Bitterly she glared at him. He had left her alone, all right. He had been patient with her, never coming near her, but it was his cold and distant disapproval which had hurt more, she thought, than anything else might have done.

'What were you thinking you should have done?' she asked. 'Beaten me?'

'That, too, perhaps,' he snapped, 'but I was thinking of this.'

Without giving her a chance to speak again, he crushed her roughly closer, and, as she lifted her chin to protest, drove his mouth down on hers in a kiss that held not one flicker of tenderness. It was a kiss which explained everything without words. It was a punishment in itself, an explicit answer to her unanswered question. It told her clearly that he considered she had never deserved his consideration, but only such treatment as he was dishing out now.

Feeling her lips being crushed against her teeth, she moaned at the pain he was inflicting, which merely appeared to incense him further. When she tried to draw back he was too strong for her. His hand clamped her head in position while his mouth prized her lips apart, as though he meant to devour them.

She was engulfed in darkness, her mouth bruised as he ruthlessly explored it, but somewhere inside her was coming to life a burning excitement which she had never experienced since Jarvis had last made love to her. She had thought it was an emotion she would never feel again and she hadn't been sorry. During their honeymoon it had often threatened to overwhelm her, making her feel wanton and unclean. Now, like a blast of hot air, it was back, making her want to forget everything and let her slender body melt and fuse with his. But again, as before, there was the deeply embedded instinct to fight it.

Then suddenly, as she began struggling weakly, Jarvis let go of her. He actually almost flung her contemptuously away from him. He was pale under his tan but otherwise undisturbed, while she was visibly swaying. She tried to speak, but a tightness in her throat wouldn't allow any words to get through. Only her heart, thumping heavily in her breast, seemed to be making any sound at all.

Jarvis spoke enigmatically. 'That hasn't convinced you that you're going to enjoy the next few days alone with me, has it?'

'No!' she cried, her eyes meeting his cold ones impotently. His mouth had hurt, but through the cruelty of his kiss he had reached a part of her which she had thought no longer existed. Yet the effect she had on him was obviously nil, and suddenly she found it utterly humiliating. He must have kissed her to confirm she meant nothing to him now, and it would only be to humiliate her further if he insisted on keeping her with him.

With a terrible clarity, she thought of the ruins of her marriage and felt strangely sick with regret. Then she remembered Sean and her regrets disappeared beneath horror. How could she have forgotten him for even a moment? 'I have to go back!' she exclaimed. 'S—someone will be looking for me . . .'

'Doesn't your fictitious lover have a name?' Jarvis asked derisively.

Fictitious lover! What was Jarvis saying? Confused thoughts tore through Linsey's head. Jarvis had kissed her, and there had been nothing gentle about the way he had done it, but she could still feel his breath on her face, still feel the masculine essence of him piercing her trembling body. She seemed filled with the scent and sound of him, ringing in her ears, flooding her lungs, as if she had been drowning in merciless, turbulent seas. He had reduced her mind to a helpless whirl, but what of his? He had sounded far from confused, but surely he couldn't suspect the truth, when she had given him no hint.

Shivering, she drew away from him, trying to avoid his close regard, which seemed to be stripping her of everything. 'Why do you talk of my—my boy-friend, as if he didn't exist?' she faltered at last.

'Because he doesn't, does he?' Jarvis said tightly.

Linsey's eyes, wide with fright, locked with his in a battle she knew she couldn't win. His voice was full of something, she wasn't sure that it was anger, but whatever it was it was sufficient to warn her of the futility of pursuing that particular line. Well, what did it matter? In a little while he must agree to taking her back to Mauritius, and, after he had taken her home, he wouldn't want to see her again. Her story had served its purpose—but how could Jarvis be so sure?

'You've been spying on me?' she exclaimed, horror in her voice as, suddenly, she came to the only logical conclusion.

'You didn't expect me not to?' he laughed coldly. 'But at least I did it myself. I could have hired a private detective to do it for me.'

She looked at him, his absolute arrogance chilling and defeating her. 'I didn't see you . . .'

'You were asleep.'

Asleep? Aghast, she remembered, 'I woke up . . .'

'I saw you stirring, in your little narrow bed.'

'But there was no one there. I looked!'

'You had no idea?'

'No, it wasn't that.' Her mind veered unsteadily. 'I sensed there was something unusual, but I thought I'd been dreaming.' Anger rose again. 'It was despicable of you!'

'We aren't involved in the most pleasing of games,' he replied curtly. 'I had to make sure that if desertion failed, I had something to fall back on.'

'And you went to make sure I was telling the truth?'

'Why so indignant?' he snapped. 'That you weren't telling the truth is very obvious. There is no man, is there?'

She shook her head.

'Has there ever been?'

'That's something you can find out for yourself,' she said sharply. 'It shouldn't be too much trouble, seeing you're so expert.'

His face went so hard she was scared. 'All right,' she babbled, somehow losing her nerve, 'you win. There hasn't been another man.'

'But now?' he smiled thinly. 'Now that the admirable Harriet has gone, there might be?'

'No!' her eyes flashed. 'As you said, some of us can do without.'

'Unless something becomes a necessity?'

'Jarvis——' Her nerves, already too taut to take much more, jumped. Suddenly she realised that while they had been talking the yacht must have moved a considerable distance. Had Jarvis kept her talking deliberately? Tersely she broke off what she was about to say, thinking of Sean, his panic if she didn't return soon.

'I want to go home, Jarvis. You can't want to keep me here any longer. You've played your little game and won. You frightened me into betraying myself.'

'You thought a lover was necessary to keep me at bay?'

'Yes,' she admitted wearily, 'if you like.'

'I don't—like!' he emphasised explosively. 'Did you really think I'd be that eager to have you in my arms again?' When she didn't speak, 'You must have done, otherwise you wouldn't have gone to such lengths.'

'Does it matter?' She was too anxious about Sean to be able to concentrate on what Jarvis was saying. Turning, to glance through the window, she saw the spill of white foam as the yacht raced ahead, and it threw her in a blind panic. Quickly she rushed towards the door.

When he caught her arm, hauling her to an abrupt halt, she aimed her open hand at his cold, hard face.

This time he was ready for her. Easily he held her until she finished struggling and slumped against him, defeated.

'That's better,' he said, almost mildly. 'I take it you're so keen to get home, you're almost ready to dive overboard?'

'Yes,' she whispered desperately, in what might easily have passed for a prayer, 'Oh, please, Jarvis!'

Her face was stark white, her eyes implored him beseechingly. What did her pride matter? It was Sean who counted. 'I'll do anything!'

'Would you?'

The silky thoughtfulness in his voice didn't register. Linsey was only aware of her own rising panic, that it was imperative she get back to Sean. When she thought of what might happen if Musetta suddenly decided to go off and leave him, she shuddered. Musetta was usually reliable, but she had a boy-friend whom she occasionally went out with of an evening, and when he called she was liable to forget everything else.

'Yes,' she replied feverishly to his softly repeated query, 'anything.'

'Well, well!' he mused with a tight smile. 'I suppose you do realise what you're saying?'

The expression on his face, while not easily definable, shook Linsey out of the trance she was in, but she felt forced to nod, even while a curious coldness encompassed her. Jarvis might be powerful and ruthless, but he was no exhibitionist, he wasn't likely to be thinking of something which might prove embarrassing to both herself and him.

But as he continued to watch her with half closed eyes she found herself beginning to tremble. 'Jarvis,' she said, when she could bear his calculating silence no longer, 'I won't fight the divorce, you know, or anything like that. It doesn't really matter about any money, and I promise I won't try and see you again. I won't pester you, if that's what you're thinking.'

'It's nothing like that,' he replied smoothly, 'so don't get alarmed. I was merely thinking of asking you to spend the afternoon with me in my cabin.'

'In your cabin?' Linsey felt stunned with shock and if it was possible she went even paler. 'I think you're teasing me! You can't really mean . . .' She swallowed and her voice trailed off, as she was unable to put her horrified suspicions into words. 'You can't really mean what I think you mean?' she whispered.

'I'm not teasing you,' he said, his eyes still expressionless. 'Jokes of this kind are not to my taste. I'm making you a proposition, that's all. If you want to get home tonight, then you have only to agree to do as I ask. It's not as if you're being asked to do something you haven't done before.'

Linsey had to fight against blind panic, to keep herself under control. 'I've never spent hours in a man's cabin before. I'm presuming it's your bedroom?'

'Correct,' he acknowledged, with an ironic dip of his head, 'but remember I'm not just any man, Linsey, I'm your husband.'

'But you're not!' she cried, flinching. 'Oh, I realise legally you still are, but that's only until we're divorced. So it doesn't really count.'

'It does with me.'

Apprehensively, she ignored this. 'What would your crew think?'

An exasperated half sigh escaped Jarvis's tight lips. 'Haven't I told you, my men are paid to work, not think. Do you imagine they're all going to walk out if they discover I'm with my wife in my cabin?'

'Oh, for heaven's sake, Jarvis,' she cried wildly, 'stop twisting everything to suit your own ends! They're bound to speculate! They must know we aren't living together.'

'I don't intend arguing with you about it,' he broke in curtly, his eyes glinting. 'I've given you an ultimatum, now it's up to you.'

Up to her! He sounded as cool as if he was discussing

a proposed tour of the islands. Didn't he know what he was asking? How could she ever agree to such a cold-blooded proposition? When he had kissed her, half an hour ago, he had displayed not a fraction of warmth. He had kissed her brutally, without emotion. She had been conscious, before he had let her go, of a certain warming of her own blood, despite the roughness of his treatment. This made her terribly apprehensive. If she did go to his cabin was it possible that, using his undoubted expertise, he could make her respond?

She remembered the depth of her response on their honeymoon, but she had changed. She was more vulnerable now, although she was older and knew she shouldn't be, but the years had wrought a difference. Jarvis was the only man she had known intimately, but she wasn't a prim, too easily shocked little schoolgirl any more. She suspected her present emotions, if properly aroused, might be capable of surprising her.

Breathing hard, she clenched her hands. As her thoughts heightened her fears rather than calmed them, she exclaimed shrilly, 'You're treating me as if I were a woman you'd just picked up off the streets!'

'There's a name for them,' he said sarcastically.

She realised he was mocking her old prudish reserve, but she merely nodded stiffly and said, 'I know.'

'Does it matter how I treat you?' he sneered. 'What makes you think you deserve more respect than the likes of them? I'd say you'd deserve all you got—and I don't have to guarantee you'll get any pleasure out of it. But then, if there's a price to be paid it's rarely pleasurable for the one who has to pay it.'

'You're despicable!' Linsey gasped.

'Somehow, your opinion of me fails to hurt,' he replied coolly.

'I'm aware of that,' she retorted bitterly, 'and that's what I can't understand. You don't like me, so what pleasure would you get if you—you took me down to your cabin? Don't tell me you'd enjoy it either?'

'You're judging this from a woman's angle,' he shrugged. 'A man is made differently.'

'You mean he doesn't have to be in love with a woman before—before . . .'

'Exactly,' he taunted softly, as Linsey's voice faltered.

With agonised eyes she stared at him, wondering if she could appeal to his better nature. 'Then you do understand how it is for a woman. You wouldn't deliberately want to hurt me?'

His eyebrows lifting cynically, he said lightly, 'I can't imagine it would be all that bad, my dear child. I think I still remember how to turn you on, even if I was never quite as successful as I would like to have been.'

Linsey flew at him then, her hand slapping his face, her own face contorted with hate and fear. 'You're a monster!' she heard herself shouting hysterically. 'I wouldn't go near you for a fortune! I hate you!' she repeated over and over again, her feet joining her hands to hit out at him furiously.

Stepping neatly aside, Jarvis avoided her, so that her foot hit only empty space and she stumbled, falling heavily. Before she hit the floor, he caught her in his arms, holding her immobile. Panting, she lay against him, her face hot with anger and panic, the terror and fright she was experiencing shining vividly from her lovely eyes.

'I won't do it!' she cried.

'That settles it, then,' he said, as she was forced to pause for breath. 'So, we cruise around for a few days, during which I promise you won't be molested.'

What was he saying? Almost on the point of collapse, Linsey's eyes widened incredulously. In her struggle to defy him she had forgotten his original plans for her. Surely he couldn't still want her with him? Swiftly she closed her eyes, thinking of Sean. She was defeated and she knew it. 'No!' she looked at him helplessly, feeling ready to die. 'I give in. Anything, as long as I get home tonight.'

'You're sure?'

Numbly she nodded.

Still he made no move, only coldly studying the agony on her face. 'You realise it will be too late to change your mind, once we're down below?'

When she nodded again, without another word he swung her slight body into his arms and carried her from the saloon.

CHAPTER FOUR

NOTHING much seemed to matter any longer. Linsey felt exhausted. She had fought Jarvis and lost and she had no strength left to fight him any more, even had she wanted to. He had defeated her, as he had often done when they lived together in London, by managing to hold the trump card. That this time he wasn't aware of what it was that had brought about her humiliating capitulation was the only thing from which she derived any comfort.

While she wished he had let her walk, she felt too frightened to try and escape from his arms. He held her closely, she presumed for her own safety, as they traversed narrow corridors and stairs. They met no one, and the silence seemed to add to her fears. The cabin to which Jarvis carried her reminded Linsey more of a bedroom in a five-star hotel. When she opened apprehensive eyes to glance quickly around she was surprised by the size and comfort of it.

Still holding her, Jarvis closed the door behind them and locked it but didn't remove the key. No one can get in and he knows I can't go out, she thought despairingly, not if I want to get home today.

She could feel his heart beating heavily against her own, but after that first swift glance around she kept her face hidden against his shoulder. To keep her face hidden and her eyes closed seemed the only form of defence left to her. If she could look on whatever might follow as a kind of punishment for being foolish enough to have allowed herself to be persuaded to dine on the yacht, it might help. Drawing a deep breath, she gritted her teeth hard in an attempt to retrieve some of the courage which was rapidly deserting her.

With her mind so tensed and ready for an immediate assault, she was stunned when Jarvis dropped her carelessly into a chair and left her there.

'If you'll excuse me for a few minutes,' he said, 'I'm going to take a shower. I was in Port Louis all morning on business and I imagine I need one. You were always fastidious, I remember.'

The breath knocked out of her, in more ways than one, Linsey stared up at him, her face white. Yet, shocked as she was, she was grateful for any kind of reprieve, however brief. She hoped he would drown in the shower. He deserved nothing less!

Then he shortened her breath again by saying mockingly, 'Why don't you try a shower yourself? You look a bit jaded.'

'I feel terrible,' she said huskily.

Ignoring this, he went on taunting her. 'If you'd rather not join me, there's another shower through that door. A bath, too, if you'd prefer that?'

His green eyes glittered down on her and she flushed at the indifference in his voice. How dared he speak to her as he was doing! 'I might wash my hands,' she answered stiffly.

'As you like,' he said dryly, as though her reply didn't surprise him. Turning abruptly, he left her to go through to the shower room. She noticed that he left the key in the main door but didn't close the door of the shower room behind him.

Bitterly Linsey gazed after him. He must be very sure she wouldn't run to his crew for help! Sitting up straighter in her chair, she glanced slowly down on her trembling hands and clenched them in an effort to pull herself together. At all costs she must remain calm. She wouldn't be the first woman to suffer the indignity of having to endure the attentions of a man she didn't want. It might just be a matter of closing one's mind to what was happening. If Jarvis were to find her a block of ice in his arms, he might conceivably have second thoughts about making love to her.

Her dazed eyes wandered around the cabin again. It was luxuriously fitted with most of the furniture screwed to the floor. An ideal love nest, she supposed, squashing a hysterical desire to giggle. Everything was of the finest quality and design. Bemused, she realised—as she expected Jarvis had deliberately planned she should—that she could have been sharing all this with him if she hadn't chosen to leave him four years ago.

The sound of a shower running jerked her eyes in this direction, and hot embarrassment flooded her as she saw Jarvis standing naked under the white spray of water. He hadn't closed this door, either, and although he had his back to her she felt immediately weak with what she took to be shocked aversion. Sharply, Linsey drew in her breath, her gaze clinging, despite her efforts to look elsewhere, to his tall, flat muscled body. His legs were long and strong, hips tautly aggressive with a suggestion of controlled strength. Even the back of his head held more than a hint of male arrogance. Swallowing painfully, Linsey managed to look away, not wishing to be caught watching if he turned around.

She made the other bathroom on legs which threatened to collapse under her, but only washed her hot face and hands. Longingly she glanced at the bath and shower, but dared not risk it. Jarvis, she knew from past experience, was quite capable of removing her from either, before she had time to put on so much as a wrap. Perhaps he wouldn't, now, but she wasn't taking any chances. After drying her hands she ran a comb lightly through her hair and returned to the cabin to sit in the chair.

Jarvis was out of the shower, she could hear him

moving about, but the shower room door was now closed. She had hoped that her wash and the breathing space he had granted her would make her feel calmer, but to her dismay she found she was still trembling. Desperately she tried a little self-derision. It wasn't as if she hadn't known Jarvis before. As he so cynically pointed out, she was no squeamish virgin, and they were married, weren't they?

When no comforting wave of reassurance followed such thoughts, she bit her lip. No amount of reasoning, it seemed, was going to make any difference. Tense with increasing despair, she shuddered. She had believed she had managed to forget she had ever had a husband, in the emotional sense, anyway. She had been confident that if ever she met Jarvis again he would be like a stranger, without any ability to stir her emotions. Now she was forced to admit bitterly this was not so, and, if anything, she was more frightened by this than by the predicament she was in at the moment. Jarvis had been capable of arousing her before, but suddenly she was aware of deep, untapped reservoirs inside her which had never been released. She was abjectly terrified of what her reactions might reveal if Jarvis really did begin making serious love to her. Silently she prayed that if he did she would be able to hang on to at least some of her habitual reserve. Never would she willingly give him the satisfaction of seeing her surrender in his arms. Hadn't he searched for her in order to get a divorce, which must prove he couldn't wait to get rid of her?

At last he re-entered the cabin and Linsey watched him with eyes made wide and dark by the trauma of her thoughts.

'Really, Linsey,' he mocked coolly, 'you don't have to look so nervous. I fully intend you to enjoy this afternoon, almost as much as I'm going to.'

Linsey, her glance travelling, hypnotised, down the

length of him again, flinched. He wore his pants, neatly belted to his waist, but no shirt, and his whole manner was relaxed, even indolent. She envied him! He was a formidable-looking man with a dark mocking face, yet at this moment it seemed he was about to purr like a tiger.

That's just what he was, she quivered, waiting for him to pounce.

He didn't do this immediately. After flicking her another cool glance he went to sit on the edge of the bed, patting the place beside him gently. 'Come,' he invited, his faintly foreign articulation very pronounced in this instance, 'you will be more comfortable here than in that chair.' When she didn't obey, remaining frozen to her seat, he commanded grimly, 'Linsey!'

If she didn't want an undignified scene then she knew she must comply, and why give him the satisfaction of a struggle? With his strength it would be one sided anyway.

Her legs felt no stronger as she stumbled towards him, if anything they were weaker, but she was oddly grateful for the numbness which was spreading over her. A momentary surge of triumph came to her. Jarvis mightn't be so pleased if he found her wholly unresponsive.

She sat down beside him still feeling beautifully numb, rather like a patient under a certain type of anaesthetic, aware of what was going on but unable to feel anything.

He turned to look at her. 'Aren't you going to speak to me?' he enquired.

'What more could I say that hasn't already been said?' she asked, dismayed to find a tremor in her voice as some of her coolness deserted her. 'Words appear to be wasted on you, and I'm not going to beg.'

'One day you might,' he said harshly, 'but for now

I'll settle for what I have to take.'

'You've always been good at taking, Jarvis.' She tried to speak calmly but couldn't keep the bitterness from her voice.

'You were never so good at giving,' he countered dryly.

Hadn't she been? Confused, she pointed out, 'I gave you what you wanted.'

'Not the way I wanted it—unconditionally. You always held back, kept a bit of yourself from me.'

'I'm sorry if you saw it that way.' She felt colour creeping up her neck, but kept her eyes fixed on the other side of the cabin.

'I had it that way,' he said coldly, 'but I'd have more sense than to accept it now.'

She didn't move or reply, there seemed no point. Looking down at her hands, she noticed they still trembled. She sat motionless, but started when Jarvis enquired silkily, 'Aren't you going to take off your dress? I'm neither young enough or old enough to appreciate undue modesty.'

'Take off my dress?'

'Unless you prefer I do it for you?' As her shocked eyes at last swung to his face, he gazed at her implacably. There was nothing in his ruthless expression to suggest he would settle for less than they had agreed on. 'We made a bargain, remember? If you change your mind I can just as easily change mine. At least within the next few minutes.'

The implications of this being too obvious to miss, Linsey was overwhelmed by panicky fright. That Jarvis seemed bent on shocking her didn't escape her, but while at another time she might have wondered why, at the precise moment there was no room in her mind for rational thought. Yet when her shaking fingers reached the front on her dress she found herself clutching it tightly to her instead of undoing the buttons.

He watched her derisively, then placed his hands on her slender shoulders, drawing her to him. 'Let me help?' he drawled mockingly.

'Don't touch me!' Her jumping nerves throwing her suddenly off balance, she immediately tried to push him away. But as soon as her frantic hands contacted his bare chest she jerked back as if she'd been stung.

Jarvis's eyes narrowed. 'I warn you, Linsey, keep on fighting me and you'll regret it.'

As his hands closed more firmly on her shrinking flesh, a look of terror spread over Linsey's white face, but she stopped struggling. She had the air of a martyr going to her doom, the hopeless, lost look of the condemned.

Jarvis's thumbs caressed the hollows beneath the bones of her shoulders as he studied her derisively. 'You didn't always meet my advances with quite so much reluctance. You don't have a lover, but is it that you're thinking of taking one, I wonder?'

This brought Linsey's chin up, her eyes blazing. 'What I have in mind is no business of yours! Physically you might be stronger than I am, but otherwise you have no power over me. I'm my own mistress.'

'Just as long as you are no one else's,' he snapped. 'Until we're divorced I won't have my name dragged through the mud.'

As she stared at him in righteous indignation, the glittering eyes bored into hers. Visibly a shiver shook her thin body as she felt again a nameless dread. Her heart was pounding and, despite his harsh words, racing with the same peculiar excitement which she had known on the beach and in the saloon. To her consternation, when her eyes met his it seemed stronger than ever, an almost tangible thing between them. And nothing, not even his most excruciating tones, appeared able to destroy it.

'Even after we're divorced,' she retorted tersely, 'I can still use your name.'

'But I'll make sure everyone knows you have nothing to do with me. After today I won't see you again.'

'I couldn't be more pleased.'

'So I must ensure,' he added coldly, as if she had never spoken, 'that you have something to remember me by.'

'But nothing pleasant?' she cried, hating him.

'It's the unpleasant things in life which I've found people appear to remember best,' he replied, unmoved.

Before Linsey could do more than gasp in protest, as if intent on carrying out his diabolical threats, he pulled her towards him, his mouth descending with a punishing ferocity. He crushed her so closely she could feel the beat of his heart and thought her body might break. His mouth burned hers, the flames he lit, scorching and merciless, and, despite the force he used, the fire grew. She felt shattered by it as tremors began tearing through her. She knew she was trembling helplessly and guessed he was aware of it, but no matter how she tried she was unable to control herself. She felt despairing that it was only by sheer concentrated effort that she was able to keep her arms rigid by her side and so prevent them from going around his neck.

Her instinct to struggle against herself as much as Jarvis was so strong that for a brief while she was able to hold herself aloof, but before he eased the cruel pressure of his mouth she was breathless and wondering how long she could hold out. She was all too conscious of melting limbs and a familiar, if almost forgotten lethargy creeping over her, which began insistently to defeat every desire she had to escape him.

Raising his head a little, Jarvis looked at her as she lay against his shoulder, taking in her hot face, her tender, bruised mouth. 'So, do you feel any differently now about taking your clothes off?' he murmured cynically.

Utterly defeated, Linsey swallowed. While she hated his tone, his silky complacency, her ability to fight him had gone. Her face feverishly flushed, her eyes half blinded by the rising tide of her desire, all she could do was to stare at him helplessly. A sob escaped her, but she made no other conscious form of protest as he took her surrender for granted and slid her dress slowly over her head. She found it impossible to even move as he pushed her back until she lay flat on the bed.

Her underclothing consisted only of a cotton bra and panties which, like her dress, she had made herself, and she would be the last to claim they were in any way glamorous. They were practical, though, so why should she close her eyes against the derision she saw in Jarvis's as he stared at them.

'Good heavens!' he exclaimed mockingly, 'they aren't exactly designed to turn a man on, are they?'

She flinched as he bent over her and her eyes flew open. 'We can't all afford the best!'

'If you'd stayed with me you could have had the best money could buy,' he taunted her.

'Do you have to keep reminding me?' she stormed, staring up at him, as fear of what was about to happen swept over her again. Suddenly all calmness left her and she twisted swiftly away from him, but before she could roll off the bed he caught her.

'Oh, no, you don't, you little cheat!' he grated furiously, one arm going round her like an iron band while his hard muscled legs trapped her own savagely beneath him.

Her breath caught in her throat as he eased himself up and bent over her again. A half strangled cry broke from her lips, but it was too late. His mouth was on hers, surprisingly the softest touch, but somehow stirring her more than his previous kisses had done. Her hands, raised to fight him, were suddenly still as the desire inside her grew. He was kissing her face, his mouth exploring the soft contours of it, then his lips lingered for a second on the pulse in her throat before returning to claim her mouth again.

As Linsey lay against him, powerless to move, she felt his strong body tauten and his hand go urgently to his belt. This was flung on the floor and she heard him groan as his mouth increased its insistent pressure. Her own softened, parting submissively, as she felt her senses flare into new and eager life. For a long, breathless minute she swung helplessly between heaven and earth, her body shuddering in his arms, her eyes closed. Then suddenly, devastatingly, he let go of her and she was free.

It took her several seconds to realise Jarvis was no longer holding her, that she lay on the bed alone. Completely bewildered, she stayed where she was, her hands going out as if unconsciously seeking him. Confused, she let them fall back to her side when she found the space beside her empty. She felt the beginnings of loss and shock, but it took the harshness of Jarvis's voice to jerk her back to complete reality.

'Get up, Linsey,' he said tersely. 'Get dressed and wait for me in the saloon. I've had second thoughts. I've decided it might be wiser to take you home.'

Numbly, her eyes wide, she gazed at him, her hot cheeks growing cold. What had happened to make him change his mind? He was savagely zipping up his pants, and she flushed as she realised how much he had wanted her.

'Do as I say, girl,' he rasped, with a brutal disregard of her feelings, 'before I change my mind again and have you instead of a cold shower.'

His contemptuous tones might have been needlessly harsh, but they succeeded in bringing Linsey to her

senses quicker than anything else might have done.
Gasping, she grasped the dress and underclothing
which he picked up from the floor and flung at her,
and put them on again. Her fingers felt all thumbs and
she couldn't concentrate.

Jarvis? Her mouth opened, but his name didn't leave
her lips. Her mouth working in agony, she tried again,
but still there was only silence. She wasn't sure if it
was shock paralysing her vocal chords, she wasn't sure
about anything. Numbly, unaware of the mute appeal
in her eyes, she stared at him.

The tension in the cabin was terrible. Linsey could
feel it around her, beating her like invisible blows. She
couldn't entirely believe yet that Jarvis was letting her
go, and while she knew she ought to be glad, she was
startled to find herself anxious about it. She wanted to
ask why he no longer wanted her, as though it was
important.

'Get out, Linsey!' His voice was low now but not
without force, and he turned his back on her.

This time she couldn't leave him quickly enough. As
she passed him she glimpsed his face. It was grim and
forbidding, but she didn't hesitate. If she had she
might have betrayed her odd desire to stay with him,
which was crazy, of course, and not to be tolerated.
She didn't know why he was letting her go, but she
wasn't stopping to ask questions. Her urgent desire to
do so faded as she fled from the cabin.

In the saloon, which she found with some difficulty,
she waited tensely for his reappearance. Fumbling in
her handbag, she found her comb and made some
attempt to restore order to her tumbled hair. Ten
minutes later she heard a noise at the door, but it was
only the steward with a tray of tea. As he placed it on a
small table in front of her she noticed there was only
one cup. but he did say that Mr Parradine had sent
word that he would be joining her shortly. And soon,

the man said, they would be putting in for the night at Port Louis again.

It was, in fact, not until they anchored off Port Louis that Linsey saw Jarvis again. The light was fading when he came to take her ashore and it was dark by the time they reached the village. Neither of them had passed more than a dozen words, and these merely ones of formal politeness. Jarvis drove her home, his face still cold and remote, obviously regretting the afternoon and disliking her intensely, yet Linsey was aware of him all the time and could think of no one else.

It wasn't until they neared the village that she realised she hadn't once thought of Sean since they had left the yacht. Scarcely able to credit this, she sat upright with a smothered gasp of dismay. Gripping the edge of her seat with tense fingers, she hoped desperately that he was all right. She didn't notice Jarvis's enigmatical glances.

When he pulled up outside the house she couldn't get out of the car quick enough. Even so, she was conscious of a painful tug of war going on inside her. Her smooth brow creased in an effort to figure it out. Half out of her mind with anxiety about her son, she wondered why she was so reluctant to leave Jarvis.

As if eager to rid herself of this latter notion straight away, she turned swiftly, only to find Jarvis's hand on her arm, delaying her.

His eyebrows were rising cynically. 'As always you like to run from me,' he said slowly, not missing the urgent little glances she was casting at the house. 'Do you realise we won't meet again?'

If she didn't she should do, for hadn't he told her so often enough? 'Yes,' she whispered, unable to look at him.

'It's goodbye, then, Linsey. I regret this afternoon but, apart from this, I'm relieved to have found you again. I'm afraid I've been content to let things drift, without much regard for—well, a certain person's feelings. Now I'll go straight ahead with the divorce, which was something I was going to explain this afternoon when I got—er—diverted. However, no harm was done and there wasn't much to explain really. If you don't fight the case I'll see you have enough to live on. My solicitor will be in touch. You won't starve, I promise you.'

Hating his dry irony as much as her own feelings of desolation, Linsey said goodbye quickly and left him. As his hand fell from her arm, she almost ran into the house. No use dwelling on what might have been. It was a little late for that now.

To her relief Sean was in bed and asleep. After gazing with blind, tear-filled eyes at his small sleeping face, she turned away, meeting Musetta as she came from his bedroom.

'What a fright you gave me, Miss Linsey!' the girl exclaimed. 'I heard a noise, but I didn't know you were home again.'

'I'm sorry,' Linsey blinked away her tears, glad of the half light, 'I should have shouted, but I was worried about Sean.'

'Sean?' Musetta shrugged. 'Oh, he's okay. He has been asking for you, though. He expected you would be home sooner.'

'I—got held up.'

'Sure . . . I told him, but you know what he is!'

Linsey couldn't suppress a wry smile. 'He doesn't usually pine for me, exactly.'

'No, Miss Linsey, it wasn't that so much,' Musetta replied frankly. 'He was bored and wouldn't be content with the sea and sand. He is not like my young brothers used to be.'

'I'll try and make up for it tomorrow,' Linsey promised automatically. Now that she knew Sean was safe, she found herself again thinking more of Jarvis.

What had he meant when he had mentioned a certain person's feelings? He must have been talking of another woman. He had scarcely looked at her as they had said goodbye. He had been a polite stranger. Was this other woman the reason why he had changed his mind in the cabin? Had he suddenly realised there could be embarrassing consequences for everyone if he went on with his folly?

Linsey still felt cold as she went to bed and she didn't sleep. The next morning, weary and sore-eyed, she was reluctant to face the battery of Sean's questions, as to where she had 'gotten to' the previous evening.

'Will you take me somewhere today?' he demanded, in his childish treble.

About to agree, Linsey remembered unhappily that she had to see Harriet's solicitor. It was merely to do with the winding up of Harriet's estate, but the appointment was already made. Her heart sank at the thought of having to go to Port Louis again, and this time she wouldn't be able to travel in comfort, as she had done in Jarvis's car.

'Sean would like to come,' Sean said, for once forgetting to use the grown-up 'I', when she informed him of her plans. 'I promise to be good.'

'Oh, darling,' she sighed, glancing uncertainly at the mutinous mouth set in an equally mutinous face. How could she explain that she dared not take him for fear his father was still there? While Jarvis had said goodbye to her, this did not necessarily mean he had left the island. Linsey was annoyed that she hadn't checked on this, but it hadn't occurred to her until now. Jarvis might possibly be staying on. And while today she could go down to the docks and see if his yacht was still there, she dared not risk bumping into him and having him catching her with Sean.

'Listen, darling,' she knelt by him, 'this is the last

time, I promise you, that I'll leave you when I'm going somewhere. Just be good until I get back. Musetta will play with you.'

'You'll be late again!' he accused her.

'Not if I can help it,' she smiled. 'Musetta wasn't able to go out with her boy-friend last night, so she's going to be very cross if I'm back late again today.'

The journey to Port Louis, as she had anticipated, proved tedious. The bus was crammed with local people and tourists and, at the height of the day, was very hot. Linsey wilted, slowly but surely. Usually she had lots of vitality, but this afternoon it seemed at low ebb. She felt unhappy and listless, as if nothing mattered much, and while usually she enjoyed the wonderful views from the bus windows, today they might have been shrouded in the thickest fog, for all the notice she took of them.

Eventually she tried to arouse herself. She would go to one of the markets and get something for Sean. Then she began worrying about what she would get. His tastes were becoming alarmingly expensive for such a small boy. No, it wasn't that, exactly, she reasoned, it was more that he liked complicated things. A toy car was no use to him unless it had an engine that really worked. A steering column and four wheels was just not good enough. Sometimes, when more because of the need to economise than anything else, she pointed out to him that such toys were made for boys of his age, he fixed her with that cold, disparaging stare which reminded her so much of Jarvis. Wistfully, Linsey sighed. She didn't think she was overly maternal, but she occasionally wished Sean had been a girl, content to play with dolls. Mauritius was so full of beautiful materials it would have been easy and a pleasure to have dressed them properly. The trouble with Sean was that he was growing up too quickly, which was depressing when she knew she would have no more children.

Why was she so sure? As Linsey left the bus she thrust such a disturbing question to the back of her mind, yet she found herself asking it again as she stared at her reflection in one of the huge plate glass windows of a shop in Royal Street, in Port Louis. How could she be so sure about something like that? It wasn't as if she was unattractive. She would have to be blind not to see the way men stared at her whenever she came here. She caught their eye and they gazed at her with desire because she was young and slender, enchanting to look at. She recognised the expression in their eyes for what it was. Even so, it had often puzzled her, if only because she was young herself, that she felt no returning flicker of interest. Maybe one day she would—or would she? Moodily she went on staring in the window.

On first arriving at Port Louis, she had called on the solicitor at the arranged hour, only to be told he had been unavoidably detained with a client at the other side of the island and couldn't see Linsey until after four o'clock. Another appointment had been made for her, if she was willing to wait. After thinking it over anxiously, Linsey had decided there was nothing else she could do, although the thought of having to spend the whole afternoon wandering alone in the town didn't appeal to her.

It did, however, provide an excellent opportunity to make very sure that Jarvis's boat was gone. She explored the docks thoroughly and could see no sign of it. There were lots of boats, though. Port Louis was such a pot-pourri of races and cultures and, although the island never seemed crowded, people visited from all over the world. A lot arrived in yachts; a lot of Mauritians owned them, too, and while Jarvis's was larger than most it might not be impossible to miss it.

At last Linsey felt desperate enough to ask two old men, obviously retired sailors, who looked as if they might have lived on Mauritius all their lives, if they had seen anything of the *Cygnet*.

'It went this morning, young missy,' they said. 'We noticed because it's a big boat. It didn't look as if it was coming back.'

They were wise, these old men of the islands. They knew boats and the men who sailed them. Without seeking official information, the advice was probably as good as she could get. With a strained smile, she thanked them.

Still uneasy, she called at the firm from which Jarvis had hired his car. It was a well known one and busy.

'Yes, Mr Parradine returned the car yesterday,' the harassed clerk told her. 'Said he was leaving. That's all I know.'

Linsey smiled and thanked him. He wasn't giving much away, but then he had a business to run. So Jarvis really had gone this time. Where was the relief she should have felt? Why did her heart feel heavy enough to weigh a ton? Wasn't she delighted to know for sure that Jarvis wouldn't be troubling her any more? Not with his presence, at least.

Not with his physical presence. Hollowly she admitted the mockery of this as the town and its inhabitants faded and she saw his darkly dominant face all too clearly. Time would help, she decided bleakly. It always had.

She started as a voice behind her exclaimed, 'Hello, there, Linsey Parradine!'

On a note of surprise she turned. It was Mark Lanier, from the sugar plantation, Mrs Lanier's unmarried son. 'Why, hello,' she answered uncertainly.

'Don't look so pleased to see me,' he grinned, but with a rueful expression in his steady blue eyes. 'Have you just arrived, or are you on your way home?'

'Neither.'

When she explained, he uttered an impatient exclamation. 'Damn, isn't that just like the thing! I have to be home to meet someone—I promised Mother. Otherwise I could have waited for you.'

'No, please,' she assured him, 'I'll be all right.'

'Tell you what,' he hadn't taken his eyes off her face, 'I have time for a cup of tea before I go. Come and have one with me. Please, Linsey?'

Because she liked him, but mostly because she was reluctant to spend the entire afternoon thinking of Jarvis, she agreed. But in the tea-shop, when he began talking about her marriage, she began to regret coming with him.

CHAPTER FIVE

'I HAPPENED to be in the village yesterday,' Mark said, 'and I saw you getting in a man's car. It's so unusual to see you with a man that I wondered if it could possibly be your husband.'

Would there be any point in denying it? Linsey thought not. She wouldn't discuss Jarvis's visit with anyone, for fear she was forced to confess she hadn't told him about his son, and that wasn't something she was particularly proud of. There could be little danger, though, in admitting that Jarvis had been to see her.

'Yes,' she replied slowly, 'that was my husband. We've been discussing a divorce.'

The blue eyes watching her quickened with interest, but he only asked, 'When?'

'I'm not sure,' she said. In a way this was true, and while she knew it would have been more honest to have said soon, suddenly she couldn't seem to bear anything quite so final. Mark wouldn't ask for any more information than she voluntarily divulged. He was that kind of person.

She had her facts right. Mark didn't push his luck, he respected her reticence, but he did place his hand over hers as it lay on the table. It was a gesture that conveyed both sympathy and affection and, somehow, she hadn't the heart to reject him.

'You know this will make a hell of a difference,' he said. 'You must have guessed how I feel about you. After the divorce I'm going to ask you to marry me, Linsey. Advance warning,' he grinned, 'but I'm going to fight for the privilege of taking care of you and Sean.'

Later, as she said goodbye to him, she didn't know whether to laugh or cry. Of course she did neither and was relieved to hear herself promising quietly to bring Sean out to the plantation one day soon. Suddenly her future was assured. Money from Jarvis and an offer of marriage from Mark Lanier. She must be one of the world's greatest fools that she felt she could take nothing from either of them. After her divorce she would be entirely on her own, but to marry Mark without loving him, even if she could bring herself to, would be wrong.

She had been annoyed when the solicitor failed to turn up for the first appointment, but she felt even worse when he was late in arriving for the second, especially when he had nothing new to tell her. Apart from one or two papers to sign, there was nothing else to do, and he only reiterated what she already knew— that the owner of Harriet's house demanded vacant possession within the next three weeks, unless the lease was renewed.

It was her own fault that she missed the bus home and had to hire a car on discovering there wasn't another bus that evening. Believing there would be another, she had wasted precious time wandering around, looking at some of the large hotels in the area, considering the possibility of finding employment in one of them. The full weight of what she was faced with hadn't really struck her until she was leaving the solicitor's office. Until then, she realised dismally, she had been subconsciously hoping for a miracle. Now the plain and very alarming facts were no longer to be cowardly put aside. She was going to have to find work and a house she could rent, if she had any hope at all of supporting Sean. Unhappily she began to understand the enormity of what she had done in not telling Jarvis about him. How could she bear seeing him having to endure poverty, which was all she might have to offer him if she couldn't find a job? Would she ever be able to live with her own conscience? Yet, while she was aware that it wouldn't be impossible to get in touch with Jarvis, she knew she couldn't do it. She couldn't bear to even think of losing Sean, for didn't she love him, and wasn't he all she had?

The hired car proved expensive and it was dark before she arrived home. She felt terribly guilty on both counts. She could ill afford the money for a bus, let alone a taxi, and Sean would be cross over her being late again. Quickly she paid the driver and thanked him, then hurried down the narrow lane which led to the house.

At the front door she was met by a hysterical Musetta. 'Sean's run away and I can't find him!' the girl cried.

'Run away?' Linsey echoed, coming to an abrupt halt, feeling herself go suddenly cold. Surely he couldn't have gone far? He was fond of playing tricks on Musetta, he might just be hiding under his bed. Swallowing an inclination to panic, Linsey tried to stay calm. 'You're sure he isn't in the house?'

'No, he is not. I've looked everywhere.' Musetta's tears flowed fast and furious, but clearly she knew what she was talking about.

Linsey's face whitened with anxiety. 'When did you first miss him?' she asked. 'What time?'

'I don't know,' Musetta wailed. 'I was getting his supper and when I shouted that it was ready, there was no reply. I had left him playing in the lounge and you know how taken up he gets with his games, but when I went to fetch him he wasn't there. Since then I've done nothing else but search for him.'

'He must be somewhere, though.' Linsey's voice was shaking, despite her efforts to control it. 'Have you looked on the beach?'

'Yes, Miss Linsey,' Musetta nodded unhappily. 'I

don't know what could have got into him, worrying us all like this. I'll whip him when I find him, the young rascal!'

Apprehensively, Linsey cut through Musetta's shrill tirade, which she knew sprang more from anxiety than anything else. Musetta loved Sean and would never lay a finger on him, not even when he was naughty and deserved to be chastised. 'How far along the beach did you get?' she asked.

'I took the torch,' Musetta whimpered, her black eyes huge, for she didn't like the dark. 'I don't know how far I got, but it seemed a long way and there was no sign of him. When I couldn't find him I thought I'd better go to the village for help. I was on my way there when you came.'

'You don't think he's gone to the village?'

'No, I don't think so,' Musetta shook her head. 'He was fretful after you left, and when he's like that he always likes to be by himself. The village would be the last place he would go to.'

'I was late,' Linsey admitted sadly. 'He must have thought I wasn't coming home.'

'He was upset when you didn't get off the last bus,' Musetta confirmed.

'We'd better begin searching again.' Linsey felt sick and wondered why she had wasted so much time already. Despairingly her eyes rested briefly on Musetta's distraught face. She felt like weeping herself, but she knew she must set some sort of example. If she broke down, Musetta would never pull herself together and that wouldn't help Sean. And, whatever happened, they had to find him!

'Musetta,' she said sharply, 'it's no use breaking down. I'm not blaming you for what's happened. I know how naughty Sean can be and I know how much you care for him, but you'll have to come with me.'

'Perhaps I can help?'

For Linsey, Jarvis's sudden reappearance, on top of a day of unhappiness and unpleasant shocks, was the last straw. 'Oh, no!' she cried, her eyes so wide with horror they seemed to swallow up the rest of her face. 'I thought you'd gone?' she gasped.

'I changed my mind.'

'But why?' She wished fervently she had heard him coming. How did he always manage to take her by surprise?

'It might have had something to do with my intuition,' he replied coolly.

'Your—what?' Linsey whispered, scarcely able to speak at all. Jarvis towered above her, talking in riddles, and she wondered if she might be going to faint. 'Your what?' she repeated, still staring at him fixedly, trying to focus his face while her head whirled.

'It doesn't matter.' Taking her arm, he gave her a reproving shake. 'There seems to be more important things to think of at the moment. Didn't I hear something about a child being missing? This girl's, I presume?'

Another wave of icy horror swept over Linsey as she realised she ought to be out looking for Sean, and that Jarvis seemed to think he was Musetta's son. Musetta obviously hadn't understood what Jarvis was saying, although she was watching him with a puzzled expression on her face. And Linsey had never told her about Jarvis arriving on Mauritius, or that he was her husband. Feverishly, Linsey hoped to be able to get rid of him before it became necessary to do so. Or before Jarvis told Musetta himself.

'You'll have to excuse us,' she tried to escape the steely grip he had on her arm. 'It's a little boy who's missing, but we'll soon find him. We don't need any help.' Fiercely she added in undertones, 'Please go away, Jarvis, and leave me alone. I want nothing more to do with you.'

His eyes hardened, but he merely stated curtly, 'I'm not going anywhere, not before the boy is found. What sort of a man do you take me for?'

As if she didn't already know! Oh, what on earth was she going to do! Almost in a frenzy, she grabbed the torch from Musetta, ordering the girl to stay where she was. Musetta was weeping too hard to be of much use, anyway, and someone ought to be here in case Sean should happen to return on his own.

Weakly she decided there could be no harm in allowing Jarvis to go on thinking Musetta was Sean's mother. Sean would soon be found, then Jarvis would go. She didn't know why he had come back, but there could be nothing to keep him here. When Sean was found she would take him straight to bed and it was unlikely that Jarvis would spare him a second glance. There was a risk, but it was small and she must be prepared to take it.

Taking Jarvis by surprise, she wrenched away from him, running swiftly in the direction of the sea. She had scarcely covered more than a few yards, however, when he caught up. 'Do you have to act like a child?' he snapped. As she shook her head wordlessly, he became coldly practical. 'Have you any idea where this youngster might be? When children, for some reason, decide to hide, they often make for a favourite spot or person.'

This made sense, Linsey realised anxiously. The trouble was she couldn't remember Sean having any particular preferences. He was over-fond of declaring himself bored with the area.

'We'd better try the beach first. He might have been playing in the sand and fallen asleep, and a small child isn't easy to see in the dark. Musetta could have walked past and never noticed him.' Linsey's hands clenched as she spoke. Sean could be hurt and crying for her. Oh, dear God!

'Where's his father, or don't you know?' Jarvis's arm shot around her as she stumbled, but Linsey was unaware of it.

'His—father?' she gasped, twisting from the stunning blow of that question so that Jarvis's hand fell from her waist. Wildly she began hurrying, as if she hadn't really taken in what he was talking about.

Sean wasn't anywhere on the beach. If he had been the wide beam of the torch would have picked him up. Thinking only of Sean now, Linsey despairingly told Jarvis, who had kept up with her easily simply by lengthening his stride. 'There are caves, but he knows they're out of bounds. They can be dangerous.'

'That kind of advice is a challenge to any boy,' Jarvis said dryly. 'It might be a good idea to take a look at these caves where he's been forbidden to go.'

'Do you think so?' Her voice trembled on the night wind.

'Lead the way.' Tersely he glanced at her, coldly thoughtful. 'This kid means a lot to you, I can see, but try to get a hold of yourself, Linsey. You're practically shaking.'

If only he knew! Going hot and cold by turns, she didn't answer.

'How old is he?' Jarvis asked, as they turned towards the caves.

'Three.' Her voice still trembled, despite her efforts to control it. Yet how could it be otherwise, with her mind reeling with such dreadful fears?

Dimly she heard Jarvis reply. 'At least he isn't a baby. Why don't you try calling him? If he doesn't see your light he might hear you.'

She had wanted to call, but her throat had been so choked with tension and distress, she hadn't been able to. Now she felt ashamed, as she realised Sean's life might be at stake.

'Sean . . .!' Her voice sounded disembodied, floating above her head, echoing through the caves as if it didn't belong to her.

'A peculiar name for an island child. Any child, come to that.'

Linsey shivered at the faint derision in his voice. 'D-don't you like it?'

'Not particularly.' He sounded bored.

He must never find out, she kept telling herself desperately.

They found Sean at last, in one of the larger caves a little farther on. He was lying on a ledge with water lapping the bottom of it. The sea didn't usually come in as far as this, and Linsey shuddered as she realised there must have been a sudden squall. She went paler still as she imagined what might have happened had the water been only a little deeper.

'Sean!' As he looked up and saw her, she plunged towards him, grasping him in her arms before Jarvis could reach him. He clung to her sobbing, for once unable to speak.

'Are you all right, darling?' she gulped, glad that the darkness must hide her own tears from Jarvis.

Sean nodded his small, dark head. 'I was frightened,' he choked against her shoulder, his thin little body trembling.

'Here, give him to me. Let me take him,' Jarvis commanded, his arms reaching out.

'No, I can manage.' Linsey hung on to Sean fiercely.

'Linsey!'

'No!' Her grip tightened so that Sean whimpered in protest. Linsey didn't hear him, she was too busy defying his father. 'Honestly, Jarvis. He knows me, and it's not as though he's injured. At least he doesn't appear to be. He often plays tricks like this,' she lied.

'Hasn't anyone told him how dangerous it is?' Jarvis

asked grimly. 'In the long run it might save you a few tears.'

'It's easy enough to criticise!' Suddenly Linsey was both angry and frightened, as well as being very wet. 'It was good of you to help, Jarvis, and I'm grateful, but this is really none of your business and I'd rather you went back to Port Louis.'

'You're in an almighty hurry to get rid of me,' he drawled, so derisively, her heart sank. It was very obvious he had no intention of leaving her immediately.

As they left the cave, Linsey prayed that Sean had suffered no real harm and she could get him to bed before Jarvis had a chance to get a good look at him. Unfortunately, in her anguish, she stumbled, and before she knew what was happening Sean was removed forcibly from her arms. Holding the boy closely, Jarvis glanced at her distraught face. 'Stop worrying,' he said, without a flicker of real sympathy. 'You'll soon be home.'

Those words, reckoned by many to be the most comforting on earth, only filled Linsey with blank despair. A muffled cry escaped her lips and she pressed white knuckles against her shaking mouth. This way she managed to keep her jumping nerves under some kind of control, but she sensed Jarvis was curious about her emotional state. Blindly she walked by his side. The moon was rising and the stars seemed to be giving off an extra quota of light. They exposed Linsey's tormented expression, if not the reason for it. Jarvis, she hoped, if he noticed her distress, would connect it with himself and her desire to be rid of him. He couldn't guess it had anything to do with Sean.

Sean's face, she saw, was mercifully hidden against Jarvis's broad chest, as though he liked the comfort of it, the sense of security it gave. She remembered how it felt to be cradled thus, herself, and she wished her heart wouldn't race so, even to think of it.

Near the house, they found Musetta searching frantically for Sean with her boy-friend. When she saw the small party approaching, she flung out her arms in excited relief. 'Oh, the young imp!' she cried. 'Where did you find him? Give him to me, monsieur,' she exclaimed, without waiting for a reply.

Jarvis ignored her coldly. 'Since I have him,' he said, 'I may as well take him into the house. He was in a cave and he could easily have drowned.'

He thought Musetta was Sean's mother and wasn't sparing her, while Musetta thought she was being chastised for carelessness, for falling down on her duties as Sean's nursemaid. Linsey had a terrible desire to laugh. Instead, with a sharpness of mind she was a little ashamed of and hadn't known she possessed, she drew Musetta quickly aside.

'I know you arranged to go out this evening,' she said. 'If you'd like to go now, I'll look after Sean.'

'But what about that man, Miss Linsey?' Musetta's voice carried. 'Do you know him? I haven't seen him around before. His face looks sort of familiar, though.'

'It's all right, I know him,' Linsey said quickly, 'and he won't be staying long.'

Musetta frowned unhappily, still not convinced. 'I could do something to help. Barbe,' she nodded towards her hovering friend, 'he won't mind waiting while I make some coffee.'

'Be quiet, both of you!' Jarvis, as though losing patience with such frantic whispering, strode past them through the open front door. Sean, wriggling in his arms, fast recovering from his ordeal, cried out for his mother.

Jarvis took the door on his right, leading to the kitchen. 'She's right behind us, young man, but you're quite safe with me.'

'I didn't mean to run away,' Sean sobbed, recognising a stronger personality. 'I only meant to get a little lost.'

'Well, you're safe now,' Jarvis repeated sternly, 'but don't do it again.'

'I'll see to him.' Linsey, having at last succeeded in persuading Musetta they could manage without her, spoke quickly behind them. Sean, she saw thankfully, was covered with sand. It was all over his face and hair. At the moment he was quite unrecognisable. He could have been anybody's child. Breathing a little more easily, Linsey tugged at his small body. 'Please, Jarvis, give him to me.'

He took no more notice of her than he had of Musetta. Instead of doing as she asked, he laid Sean carefully down on the long kitchen bench they often used as a seat. Contemplating him ironically, he said, 'Possibly all he needs is a good wash and his bed, but before I go I must satisfy myself that he isn't injured in any way. He's not very old and could easily have broken a bone without realising it.'

'Of course he hasn't!' Words tumbled urgently from Linsey's taut lips. 'Children fall soft, it's well known, they never break bones. I'll soon have him cleaned up, but before I start I can see you out. Oh, and if you want to see me again I'll come to Port Louis.'

Jarvis didn't move. Ignoring what she said, his glance flickered from her pallid face to the empty doorway. 'Where's that girl gone?'

'Musetta?' Nervously Linsey looked away from him. 'She's had to go out. A social gathering . . .'

'Some mother!' he snapped. 'You shouldn't encourage her.'

'I don't . . .' Too late, Linsey wished she had thought of a better excuse.

With a dismissive shrug, Jarvis was at the sink, despite her protests, filling a dish of warm water and reaching for a flannel, his intentions obvious.

'I'll do it, he's used to me.' Linsey tried to take the dish from him. Defiant blue eyes clashed with glittering green ones and for a moment the world stood still as their glances locked.

Sean, sensing tension in the air, began howling again.

Linsey bit her lip painfully while Jarvis spoke to Sean sharply. Sean immediately stopped making a fuss and raised his head. 'That's better, my lad,' Jarvis approved softly, getting busy with the soap and water.

There was nothing left for Linsey to do but start praying to her guardian angel who, unfortunately, didn't seem to be around right then. Despair almost paralysing her, she watched, in a kind of trembling state of suspense, as Jarvis began washing the caked sand and grime gently from Sean's face. Slowly but surely it emerged, a perfect replica of Jarvis's own, if not quite so strongly hewn. Men were supposed to be blind, weren't they? Linsey reasoned wildly. The light wasn't very good. Perhaps Jarvis wouldn't notice.

He didn't, not for the first few minutes, as he grimly pursued his self-appointed task, ignoring Sean's whimpers as the removal of the sand occasionally scratched his skin.

'Let this be a lesson to you, young man,' Jarvis's voice was stern, but this time held a note of quiet humour. 'If you have a thirst for adventure wait until you're grown up, or at least until your father can spare the time to go with you.'

At this, Sean raised puzzled eyes to frown at him, and it was then, as she heard Jarvis draw a rough, incredulous breath, that Linsey knew the game was up. For a long moment she seemed to hear nothing but the harsh sound of Jarvis's breathing, but it must have been partly her own panic which filled her ears, screaming in her head, like a demoniacal symphony out of control.

Then, like the final crash of discordant notes, came Jarvis's voice. 'Mine!' he rasped, slamming the accusation right at her, like a shot from a gun. His face flushed red then went white under his tan. 'You lying bitch!' Her turned to stare at her with hate in his leaping eyes. 'This boy is mine. He's my son!'

He wasn't asking her, she realised dully. There was no doubt in his mind that he was Sean's father, he wasn't going to allow her to deny it. He was staring at her, his green eyes glittering darkly. Instinctively she shrank back. The catastrophe she had always dreaded but thought would never arrive was not only here, but much worse than ever she had imagined it would be.

When Sean, stirring restlessly, cried, 'Mummy?' and she automatically took hold of his hand, it appeared to cap Jarvis's moment of dreadful triumph.

She saw, from the black anger on his face, that he was incensed, and she couldn't honestly blame him. It must have been a soul-shaking experience to have seen a mirror-like reflection of his own face in Sean's. And for a man like Jarvis to suddenly discover he had been a father for over three years and never known must have been a terrible shock, as well as a blow to his pride.

She recalled his family, his continental relations, their almost fanatical pride in their ancestry, and their descendants, and marvelled that she had ever believed Jarvis would be willing to reject his.

Swallowing an outsize lump in her throat, Linsey was suddenly aware of the magnitude of her sins. For it must be a sin to keep all knowledge of a son from his father. Harriet had advised her not to get in touch with Jarvis, but she thrust this impatiently aside. The time was past for excuses, for hiding weakly behind the superior strength of others. She ought to have had the courage to make her own decisions. What if Jarvis had been in love with another woman? Two wrongs didn't make a right, did they? And Jarvis's crime was surely nothing to the one she had committed? From now on, although she could never bring herself to give Sean up, she must do everything possible to prove she was sorry for what she had done.

Jarvis had returned to studying Sean's face, but she had seen the hatred and contempt in his eyes when he had looked at her. Yet when he glanced at her again the hatred was gone and she wondered if she could have been mistaken.

His voice was as expressionless as his face as he reminded her flatly, 'You haven't actually answered my question.'

Beyond deviousness, she whispered hollowly, 'Yes, he is your son.'

Sean's whimpering cry filled the taut silence that followed Linsey's trembling confession. He asked if he could have a drink and go to bed.

Wordlessly, feeling almost too frightened to move now without permission, she looked at Jarvis.

'Yes, take him,' Jarvis already seemed to be taking command. 'He'll be better in bed. When we talk I want no interruptions.'

Scarcely knowing what she was doing, Linsey made Sean a warm drink which he was almost too weary to swallow, then carried him to his room. Jarvis made no further attempt to touch him, but he followed and watched as she laid Sean in his cot.

Linsey glanced at him quickly. Was he comparing this room with what Sean might have had, had he lived at Worton Manor with him? Or was he making sure she didn't run away? Bleak despair filling her to the exclusion of everything else, she wished, momentarily, that there was somewhere she could run to, if only to hide her head. Her mind was so choked with indefinable fears that she knew, if Jarvis attacked her, she wouldn't be able to think straight.

Sean turned over and snuggled down, murmuring sleepily, 'I'm sorry, Mummy, sorry I ran away . . .'

His voice trailed off as she bent to kiss him and cover him with a sheet. She added a blanket, fearing he might be cold after his ordeal. Anxiously she lingered, gazing down on him as he closed his eyes. Her relief on finding him had been partly eclipsed by Jarvis's presence and all it might mean, but now she realised how utterly thankful she was that he was safe.

Tears stung her eyes and she blinked them away as Jarvis moved nearer and once more stared down at Sean. Because his face still held little expression, she tried to concentrate her own attention on their son. What would Sean say when he discovered he had a father, because of course Jarvis would make sure he found out. She felt a twinge of something very like jealousy when she suspected Sean would be pleased. Jarvis was the kind of man any boy might be proud to call his father.

So distressing were her thoughts that she actually welcomed Jarvis's tug on her arm and his curt reminder that they had things to talk about. He spoke softly, but the hint of menace in his voice brought her fears rushing back. It wouldn't be just a divorce he wanted to discuss this time!

'Couldn't we talk in the morning?' she implored, despising herself for being a coward but unable to help it.

'No!' When she would have desisted, he shook his head contemptuously and drew her forcibly through to the lounge.

Once there, he let go of her arm while he closed the door. Stumbling to a chair, Linsey sat down, feeling if she didn't her legs might collapse under her. Her eyes, wide with fatigue and the helpless despair of the cornered, fixed on Jarvis as he relentlessly pursued her.

He didn't prevaricate or allow her to. 'Why didn't you tell me?' he asked, his eyes hard on her chalky face.

'You mean about Sean?' Linsey knew she was blatantly playing for time, and was a fool to do so, but the explanations which she guessed Jarvis was about to demand were too painful not to try and avoid if possible.

'It's no use, Linsey,' he snapped, his voice flinty with impatience. 'You never did like facing the truth, but you may be sure I'm demanding it now. I want to know about my son, and I intend to know, even if we stay here all night! I want to know why you chose not to tell me about him. Surely you must have realised I had the right to know?'

How dared he ask such a question? Forgetting she had meant to be humble, Linsey succumbed to a surge of anger. 'I think you forfeited your rights,' she choked.

'Forfeited them!' he muttered some epithets which made her cheeks burn. 'How the hell could I do that? All these years I've been unaware I had a son! You were supposed to have lost the baby!'

'I almost did,' she whispered, flinching under the contempt in his eyes. 'And that,' she added wildly, 'was your fault.'

'My fault?' His fury leapt, annihilating hers. 'No matter what you care to believe, I repudiate that.'

What about the other woman? she whispered silently. The nights you spent away from home? The worse ones which you spent at home and never came near me? But none of this escaped her numb lips as he went relentlessly on.

'If anyone was at fault, Linsey, it was you. If anything brought on a miscarriage—or a threatened miscarriage, as it appears to have been now—it was your own over-emotional state. You spent too much time mourning your parents. Grief is natural and understandable, but you made a feast of yours. You seldom thought of me, the nights I sweated for you and was ignored. You didn't want anything to do with me, but I made an ideal scapegoat.'

'It wasn't like that . . .'

'If you say so.' His mouth curled in a face all harsh, cold angles. 'So let's leave that for the time being and get back to my son. To the beginning—or should I say, his beginning?'

As colour swept hotly under her clear skin, he became savagely furious. 'I didn't intend going back that far, but perhaps we should recap? You might really have good cause to blush if you recall the night you spent in my arms and we never slept. The only night I wouldn't let you. Then the morning, a few weeks later, when you were so sick there could only be one conclusion!'

'Don't!' she begged, pressing demented hands over her burning cheeks, amazed at his cruelty. What good did he think it would do, reminding them both of things which were better forgotten?

As if he had already forgotten, Jarvis pressed on. 'That fool of a doctor! Or was it you who somehow fooled him?' His eyes narrowed in sudden suspicion. 'He was an eminent man, the best in the field. He couldn't have made a mistake.'

'Don't you remember?' she asked bitterly. 'He told you he feared I'd lost the baby, but you didn't wait for him to finish.'

'You knew I was already late for an urgent appointment!'

'Another merger!' when she had been aching for the comfort of his arms. 'You thought business more important.'

'It paid for a lot of things you were rapidly beginning to take for granted,' he retorted coldly.

'Well, never mind.' Perhaps he was right, she felt too taut to argue, 'You didn't wait to hear how Mr Jardine suddenly felt ill as he began examining me, and said he'd better return to Harley Street and send his colleague. Unfortunately, as you know, on the way back there he was involved in an accident and died. It was discovered he'd had a brain haemorrhage. I told his partner, afterwards, about Mr Jardine feeling ill, and he said it all tied in.'

Jarvis frowned. 'So he wouldn't have had time to make any notes on your case, and that was why no one else came?'

'Didn't you wonder about it? Why I wasn't sent to hospital, or had no more medical care?'

'No,' he replied tautly. 'Maybe I should have done, but I didn't think it was all that serious. I knew you couldn't have been more than a few weeks pregnant, and you didn't seem at all ill.'

'That was because I hadn't lost the baby. It was only because I was young and ignorant, and because of what the doctor had said, that I feared I had. A week or so later, when I began to have suspicions, I went to see a strange doctor privately and he confirmed I hadn't lost anything. I'd had a threatened miscarriage, that was all.'

'You little bitch!' Jarvis snarled, for the second time in half an hour, but this time bending over her to grasp her arms. 'You discovered that, and not only did you think I had no right to know, but you ran off and left me! And you never intended coming back to me, did you? Otherwise you wouldn't have come all the way here. Heaven help me!' his eyes glittered with fury, 'I feel like hitting you, Linsey. I'm having some difficulty in restraining myself! Why did you do it?'

CHAPTER SIX

WHY had she done it? Looking back, she decided she must have been a little deranged. It was an incredible step to have taken, but it was difficult after four years to recall some things very clearly. She did remember, though, the desperate need she had felt to find Jarvis and tell him the good news. She had been going to ask if they could make a fresh start. Her heart had been full of apprehension, but there had also been hope.

Gazing at him now, at the unconcealed hate in his eyes, she knew she couldn't explain about going to his office and finding him with Olivia James. If she did he would realise how she felt about him—or, she corrected herself hurriedly, how she had felt about him then. She had just lost her parents and, according to the second doctor, almost her baby, yet her despair on those occasions, though great, had been nothing to that which she had known on discovering Olivia in Jarvis's arms. Knowing she had lost him seemed worse than anything she had experienced before. She had felt hopeless and beaten, with only one thought in her head, to get away.

'I thought our marriage was finished,' she replied at last, knowing this was partly the truth, 'and I didn't want you to feel obliged to stay with me because of the baby. I imagined you would see it as a kind of blackmail and hate me for it, for trying to hold you this way.'

'You must have been crazy,' he snapped, 'to think I wouldn't want my own son.'

She noticed he made no mention of herself. 'I didn't doubt you would marry again,' she said, thinking bleakly of Olivia.

'How did you imagine I was going to be able to do that, when I was still married to you?'

His jeering tone jolted her, but she tried not to let him see. 'I believed you would divorce me for desertion. Harriet said you could do so easily and that I needn't know.'

'Your friend Harriet appears to have been an authority on a lot of things she knew nothing about,' he retorted coldly, 'but it seems you were eager enough to listen.'

'She was the only one I had to listen to.'

His mouth hardened, but otherwise he betrayed little of the extent of his anger. 'So you got here,' he said grimly, 'and settled in comfortably. Then, after a few months, my son was born and still you didn't think it was your duty to inform me?'

'You would have taken him,' she cried, her eyes widening with fear as she remembered he still could. 'Harriet . . .'

'Yes?' he prompted silkily. 'Harriet said?'

'Nothing,' Linsey muttered defiantly, guessing his opinion of Harriet. Irrationally she added, unable to restrain herself, 'But she was right, wasn't she? You would have taken him?'

'Naturally.'

The shock of his blatant admission whitened her face, although it was something she had always known. 'How can you say that when you never really tried to find me?'

'We're talking about my son.'

He kept talking about his son, as though determined to remind her! Nervously, filled with a nameless dread, she looked at him. Was there any sense in making one last bid? 'You don't have to worry about Sean, Jarvis. I won't stop you from seeing him again, but he belongs to me.'

'Really, my dear,' his head snapped back in total derision, 'your generosity overwhelms me.'

'I'll fight you for him, if I have to,' she felt driven to threaten.

Again, Jarvis merely jeered. 'And what will the courts have to say, I wonder, when they compare what I have to offer against what you've got? They'll be laughing their heads off. Even without that non-exist-ent commodity, your conscience, you have no case.'

'You're insulting!' she whispered.

'And hard,' he voiced her unspoken thoughts cyni-cally. 'I can also be a lot of other unpleasant things which I'm sure you wouldn't like any better, if you insist on fighting me over Sean.'

If he intended divorcing her surely he realised she would try and fight for his custody? 'I'm his mother!' her voice changed imploringly. 'I love him, Jarvis, I always have. I really suffered when he was born. You can't know how much, because you weren't here.'

'As I recall, you denied me that right,' his eyes narrowed coldly on her slim, seductive figure. 'If you'd given me any inkling of what was happening I assure you I would have been right by your bedside.'

Linsey shivered, her face colouring, as she wondered what that would have been like. Too late, she realised she would have given anything to have had him there.

'You're still a little prude, aren't you?' When she made no reply, he judged her rising colour mistakingly. 'My God,' he added, 'you won't be this time, before I'm finished with you!'

His tone did nothing to stop Linsey shivering. She wanted to ask what he intended doing next, but couldn't find the courage. She had a feeling that she was seeing Jarvis clearly for the first time, seeing something of his ruthlessness and grim determination. His face was handsome, but so unforgiving she was almost afraid to look at him.

'What made you come back here tonight?' she questioned, unaware of her hunted expression. 'It couldn't have been because you'd found out about Sean, or you'd have said so as soon as you arrived.'

His green eyes glittered with cruel satisfaction. 'You won't want to believe this, but it was the way you went on yesterday that made me suspicious.'

'The—the way I went on?'

'Yes, on the yacht.'

Why didn't he explain instead of tormenting her like this? Bewildered, she stared at him. 'What did I do to make you suspicious?'

'You went with me to my cabin, you were willing to do anything I asked.'

Still she didn't understand what he was talking about. 'It wasn't my fault that you practically threw me out. I agreed—I'll admit I didn't want to, but you can't accuse me of going back on my word.'

'That's just it,' he said silkily, 'you didn't want to, no more than I did.' At her soft gasp, he asked savagely, 'Did you really believe I wanted you, and so much I couldn't wait?'

Linsey felt she had been struck and the pain strained her voice. 'Then why?'

His eyes flickered at her obvious agitation, with a hint of gratification. 'I took you to my cabin merely to see how far you were prepared to go. When I asked you to lunch on the yacht it was for personal reasons which we needn't go into, but you made such a fuss I began to wonder why you were so frightened.'

'How did you know I was frightened?' she faltered. 'I tried to hide it.'

'Not very successfully, though,' he mocked. 'And somehow I couldn't believe you were all that nervous of me. There had to be another reason. Your apprehension began to intrigue me and I'm afraid I began teasing you, but what started on my part as a little game soon took over my imagination. I became very curious to know why you were so desperate to get home. Suddenly it wasn't a game any more. All my instincts told me I was on the brink of discovering something important. I was unable to ignore the feeling. It was that which made me push you as far as I did.'

Linsey's cheeks burned. 'So that charade in your cabin was all part of an act?'

He shrugged coolly. 'It began that way, as part of a plan to extract information. A plan which probably developed on over-dramatic lines, but at the time it seemed necessary.'

'So you didn't actually—desire me?'

Glancing at her bent head, he smiled cruelly. 'I could have taken you, but only because you're a very attractive woman.'

She flinched at that and was forced to answer with pride. 'Did you never suspect what was making me desperate enough to give in to you?'

His mouth hardened at her sharper tones, but he shook his head. 'I thought it was a lover. You said you hadn't one and I believed you'd lied to me. That was why I was incensed. I'm afraid I still think there might be a man somewhere, but on the yacht it was Sean you were worried about, wasn't it?'

'Yes,' she confessed bleakly. 'How could I tell you about him when you might try to take him away? And I knew how terrified he would be if I suddenly disappeared.' A peculiar exhaustion attacked her as their eyes met. 'You were so sure it was another man, it seemed a good way out, but that doesn't explain why you're here tonight.'

'My curiosity was still unsatisfied.' A slight frown accompanied his words as he recalled his own impatience at being unable to ignore this. 'When I tried to forget it, it only grew stronger. In the end I decided it might be amusing to do a little private snooping.'

'That was nice of you!' Linsey jeered. 'But isn't that what you've been doing, ever since you came here?'

Jarvis's glance smouldered. 'Since I came to Mauritius my intuition has probably been working overtime, but it certainly paid off.'

'For you, yes,' she conceded bitterly. 'And you must have had fun. You pretended to leave . . .'

'I didn't pretend to do anything. I simply sent my crew off on the yacht for a few days while I stayed behind to investigate you. I gave no reason and they didn't ask for one.'

All the same, she was sure he had done his best to cover his tracks. 'So, in your role as a great detective, what did you find out? Before you arrived, that is?' she asked sarcastically.

His mouth tightened warningly. 'I saw you kissing a man outside a teashop, for a start.'

'You really threw yourself into it, didn't you?' she returned tersely. 'The man you saw was Mark Lanier, a neighbour, and he was kissing me. It was the first time—and he isn't my lover!'

'While you are my wife,' he sliced in, 'I won't have you making a public exhibition of yourself.'

Linsey didn't tell him that Mark had asked her to marry him, because she feared Jarvis's temper. Not for herself so much as Mark. She wouldn't put it past Jarvis to confront him, and the Laniers were a dignified family.

'About Sean——' Jarvis, to her surprise, changed the subject abruptly, as if a warning would suffice. 'To learn that I have a son comes as something of a shock, but from now on I'll be responsible for him. He comes with me.'

Not content with spying on her, he was now going to deprive her of Sean. Or he was going to try to! Her fighting spirit aroused, Linsey protested, 'I won't let you take him away from me. It's not as if I can't look after him.'

'How well can you?' Jarvis asked grimly, deflating the optimism she had scraped together with one withering glance. 'Have you any money? Did this Harriet woman leave you a thing?'

She shook her head.

'This house,' he pursued relentlessly, 'does it belong to you?'

'No . . .'

'You're living in it? Does Mark Lanier pay for it?'

Again she shook her head, but the scepticism in his eyes forced her to confess, 'The owner wants us out.' She didn't know why she was telling him this; by doing so she could be signing her own death warrant.

'Where had you planned to go?'

'I hadn't.'

'You mean,' he was harshly incredulous, 'you have nowhere? No money, no house—do you even have a job?'

Slowly she shook her head, thinking how nice it would be if she could nod it for a change. Flatly she said, 'I was looking for a job. That's what I was doing in Port Louis today, as a matter of fact. I'm thinking of applying to one of the big hotels.'

Running his eyes over her curvaceous figure, he drawled insolently, 'I'm sure some man would take you on, but what about Sean?'

'Musetta, the girl you thought was his mother, will take care of him.'

'While you earn enough to keep the three of you?' His glance was still insolent as it traced the outline of her rounded breasts. 'There's only one kind of job I can think of that would enable you to do that.'

'I—I don't care what I do!' she retorted furiously, deliberately reckless. Let him think what he liked! What he was thinking was obvious enough, but she didn't care! 'At least I'd be able to look after Sean during the day.'

'Never!' he snapped. 'You can forget about that. Sean comes with me—you, too, if you like.'

'Me?' Linsey's eyes rounded.

'I'm giving you the chance.'

'You—you can't really mean it?'

'I never say things I don't mean, Linsey.'

As the hardness of his voice appeared to criticise her integrity more than his own, she bit her lip. The unexpectedness of his offer shook her, but she found it difficult to believe he was asking her to live with him again. Her heart leapt at the prospect, then steadied dully. There was too much bitterness between them, surely, to make a resumption of their married life possible.

'I——' she hesitated, 'I'm not accusing you of being insincere, Jarvis. I just thought you might be making an idle remark.'

'In a conversation like the one we're having, one doesn't make that kind of remark,' he said coldly.

He stared at her as he spoke, but she was so confused she looked away from him. There had been something in his eyes, but in an instant his expression had shifted. It was as if he had pulled a shutter over his real feelings. When she glanced again the flicker of hate she had imagined was gone. Not a sign of animosity showed on his face. Whatever had been there was now replaced by a surprising tolerance.

Startled but encouraged by it, she whispered, 'Why are you offering to have me back?' She had to know before she committed herself. Though dazed and not altogether in control of her feelings, she was sensible enough to realise her whole future might depend on the outcome of the next few minutes. 'You're sure,' she added, 'you're not being too hasty?'

'I don't always make lightning decisions,' he said

curtly, 'but I believe I might be right in making this one. Sean must love you, you're his mother, so it stands to reason he might suffer if he was suddenly taken away from you. Until he has time to settle down it might be wiser if you and I were together.'

'Together?'

His eyes narrowed as he bent a closer scrutiny on her deepening colour. 'If you mean in the fullest sense of the word, I don't think so. But who knows, in time . . .' he allowed his voice to trail off suggestively.

Linsey, despite a whispering of inner caution, felt strangely reassured. Jarvis had been murderously angry that she had deceived him over Sean. But apparently, like herself, he was trying to be sensible and put his anger aside. It must be a step in the right direction that he was beginning to consider things from someone else's point of view. A short while ago she had feared he was about to remove Sean forcibly and make sure she never saw him again, but something seemed to have changed his mind. He must have had second thoughts? Or had he? Warily, her mood swinging like a pendulum, she halted the grateful utterances about to fall from her lips. Instead of being too impulsive, perhaps she should give herself time to think.

'Linsey?' He had let go of her arm. Now he straightened away from her, running a cynical hand around the back of his neck. 'Your hasty decisions in the past haven't been exactly beneficial to anybody, so I'd rather you slept on this. I don't want you to feel I'm rushing you, and if you do agree to come back to me I won't let you change your mind. There's still a lot to discuss but nothing that can't wait until morning, when we might both be feeling better.'

Linsey was forced to agree he was right. And she would need to feel better, to make sure he didn't have some devious plan up his sleeve. Fully aware of his shrewd intelligence, she realised this was possible. Like he said, it mightn't do to be too hasty. Resisting a feminine urge to have everything settled immediately, she rose to follow his advice.

Briefly nodding her head, she said, 'I'll just take a quick look at Sean, then go to bed. Whereabouts are you staying in Port Louis, Jarvis?'

'At a hotel, but I'd rather sleep here.'

She flushed, feeling his contemplative gaze on her. 'Oh, but . . .' she began protesting defensively.

'Not with you.' His mouth twisted. 'Not yet, anyway. We would need to be very much in love before we shared a bed your size. I was thinking you must have a spare room, now your friend's gone.'

'Harriet's?' She tried to take no notice of his taunting tone. She would rather he was out of the house, but he might not take it kindly if she asked him to go. 'I'm afraid Harriet's bed is almost as small as mine. I'm sure you would be much more comfortable in Port Louis.'

'Linsey!' he suddenly lost patience. 'For me, at the moment, there are more important considerations than comfort. Whether you like it or not, I'm staying with you. Just give me a couple of clean sheets and a pillow. You're dithering about bed like you did on our wedding night. Or don't you remember?'

How dared he remind her of that? A few minutes later, after Jarvis had closed his bedroom door firmly in her face, Linsey stumbled blindly to her own room and, after getting quickly undressed, lay down, staring at the ceiling, trying not to remember.

Like Jarvis, she had more important things to think of. Sean, for instance. How would he react when he learnt that Jarvis was his father? Would he be pleased? Suspecting he would be, she felt both hurt and resentful. Jarvis had mentioned their wedding night, she didn't know why, but he appeared to have every intention of taking over in the morning, just as authoritatively as he had done then.

Unwillingly she recalled everything that had happened after she had agreed to marry him, the way in which he had arranged everything from beginning to end. He'd had no objections to a white wedding just as long as it didn't hold anything up. He refused to wait.

Despite anxious protests from Linsey's father, who had thought she might be too young to know her own mind, they had been married within a few short weeks. Linsey's mother, convinced that her daughter was making a brilliant match, was in her element, while Linsey, in a daze, had scarcely got used to wearing her engagement ring before it was joined by an equally expensive gold one. Everything about the wedding had been expensive. Jarvis, naturally, being able to afford the best, had insisted on it, even to her wedding dress. This had been a model costing hundreds of pounds and so beautiful she was almost afraid to wear it. He had paid for it all, sweeping aside parental objections, as he had known Linsey's father wasn't a rich man. He had entered her life like a strong spring tide sweeping all before it, and so he had remained.

On the whole, Jarvis had been charming to her parents, and if occasionally she wished he might have shown a little more tact, she was content in the knowledge that they liked him. On the day of the wedding all dissension was forgotten and she had walked up the aisle, a beautiful bride. Jarvis had turned deliberately to stare at her as she approached. Impressively handsome and formidable, with his dark head thrown back, he had almost stopped her breath. His eyes had remained on her face and stayed there, even after she reached his side. A tiny muscle had jerked in the tenseness of his jaw. Funny, how she remembered that almost more clearly than anything. Her hand trembled as she placed it in his. 'With this ring I thee wed . . .'

he had vowed, and again the muscle had jerked.

He hadn't seemed to let go of her hand for the rest of the day—an exhausting if wonderful day, which culminated in a honeymoon, something which Linsey knew now she hadn't been ready for. The glamour of a big wedding, the bustle and excitement leading up to it, yes. With her abundance of youthful energy and vitality, she had taken the preparations in her stride. It was on the emotional side she couldn't quite cope. She loved Jarvis, but he hadn't ever said he loved her. If she hadn't been so entirely ignorant she might have wondered. Having had so little to do with men, she had easily mistaken passion for love. This, she had realised bitterly, later, was the plain, unvarnished truth. Jarvis had wanted her, he had been prepared to go to any lengths to get her, but he wasn't prepared to pretend he loved her.

On the journey to their sundrenched honeymoon island, his patient restraint had diminished. The expression in his eyes as he glanced at her had made her very conscious of his desire and frightened by it. She began to realise the gap, not only in their ages but in experience. Jarvis was handsome enough even without the additional attraction of a superb physique. Six foot three of hard-packed muscle was enough to make any girl's heart beat faster, but Linsey's senses had suddenly refused to react. Or had overreacted, she wasn't sure which. All she recalled was the state of her nerves as Jarvis and she had entered the luxury villa, lent to them by one of Jarvis's foreign relatives. This relative, who used the villa only for holidays, owned the whole island. They had it to themselves.

'We're fortunate,' Jarvis sighed with satisfaction. 'At least, I am,' he had amended gallantly, turning to gaze once again on his beautiful young bride.

Linsey had wanted a leisurely bath before supper, then a slow getting ready for bed. All these things might be unnecessary in Jarvis's eyes, but surely he didn't expect her to be eager to go straight to bed?

It seemed he did. He had taken her in his arms, murmuring that he wanted her and couldn't wait. He had kissed her with increasing passion until Linsey, cold with fright, wriggled away from him. When she insisted wildly on a bath, he had given in with a quirk of good humour which had surprised her, until she learned the reason for it. She had been in the bath no longer than five minutes when he came and scooped her out of it.

Dripping wet, she had felt none of the instant languor of story-book heroines. 'You'll get soaked!' she had cried, in outraged indignation.

He was wearing a silky robe and had laughed at her flushed agitation. 'It doesn't matter. I have nothing on underneath.'

'I'd like a chance to put something on!' she had hissed between her teeth.

'You don't need anything.'

Desperately she had pleaded that she was hungry. Although holding her closely in his arms, Jarvis still managed to survey every inch of her. 'So am I for you,' his voice slurred as he lowered his head to crush her trembling mouth. His breath had been hot on her face, his eyes dark with leaping lights. Linsey remembered seeing flames in his eyes before, when he had kissed her at Worton Manor, but these flames were different. They indicated a man not attempting to control the raging fire from which they were blazing.

Had he tried? Uneasily Linsey stirred. It was his wedding night and his bride had been as eager for marriage as he. She was a virgin, but what did that mean nowadays? Girls didn't tremble and get hysterical any more. They knew what they were doing—what they wanted. She had wanted Jarvis, she still wanted him, she told herself, only not like this!

'Don't stiffen up on me, Linsey,' from the censure in his voice he might have read her thoughts. 'You married me with your eyes open, so don't try and cheat.'

'I'm not,' she had cried, near to tears.

She had tried to hide her distress, not quite knowing the reason for it herself, but he had seen her tears and been infuriated by them. 'If you believe you can play the outraged virgin with me you're making one hell of a mistake!'

He began kissing her again, then, when she had stopped fighting, carried her through to the bedroom and flung her on the bed. The plea that she didn't mean to deprive him of his rights died on her bruised lips as she had opened dazed eyes and watched, with startled apprehension, the swift removal of his robe. She had been ashamed of her own nakedness but, at the same time, glad she wouldn't have to suffer the indignity of having her clothes torn from her body—something which Jarvis, in his temper, looked quite capable of doing.

Without his robe he was as naked as she was, and she hadn't been able to suppress a low cry of fear. She had never known a man like this before and her mind, already taut from a day exhausting for any girl, refused to let her calm down, to see things rationally. He had moved closer, the lean body hard and tense. As he lowered himself beside her and his hand touched her breast, she had heard the fierce intake of his breath. One word of humour, perhaps of love from her, might have calmed the savage beast into which she was convinced her husband was changing. As it was she had tried to escape him by rolling off the other side of the bed, then hitting out at him when he had followed her to the floor, all the time fighting the sensuous invasion of his mouth until he had completely lost patience.

In the end he had taken her ruthlessly with no regard

for her frantic whimpers. His excitement becoming intense, he hadn't shown her any mercy. He had been so rough with her, she had been stunned. She hadn't expected to have to fight the sudden swift arousal of her own body. Her fear of this almost as great as her fear of Jarvis, she had begged him, in broken whispers, if he couldn't stop, to be gentle.

'I might have been,' he muttered thickly, his body invading hers, 'but it's too late now.'

She hit out at him as his weight crushed her, tearing her apart. In a frenzy of panic she had struggled, but could do nothing against his superior strength. The pain had remained, growing, enveloping her. She hadn't been able to understand the eventual force of her own response. It was something she hadn't expected or been able to control. On the other occasions which had followed, during the course of their brief honeymoon, she had been prepared and steeled herself against betraying too much ardour, but on her wedding night, that first time, it had been like a leap into space, with the world spinning and no holding back.

The next morning Jarvis had apologised and, though she sensed his regret, there had been no real remorse in his eyes. It didn't surprise Linsey that even before the news of her parents' death had arrived, there had been a rift between them. She supposed they had both tried to put things right, but it hadn't been easy. The rift had remained and widened. If she went back to Jarvis now, he wouldn't demand his marital rights, but living with him would be a strain. It had been before and she didn't think anything had changed. Jarvis looked older, but he would always be a very attractive man. He affected her oddly. She hoped that didn't mean she still had some feelings for him. The only thing she could be certain of was that he had never loved her. Not one word of love had ever escaped his lips all the time she had known him. Yet, for Sean's sake, she knew she had no other alternative but to return to London with him.

Linsey was down on the beach with Sean when Mark Lanier called. Jarvis had gone to Plaisance airport to collect Sean's new nanny off a plane. Jarvis, with an ease which still astonished her, had arranged everything down to the smallest detail. The new nanny would go straight to the yacht, and tomorrow they would all leave here and join her. The house would be handed back to its owner and a chapter of Linsey's life would be closed.

Sean was already missing his father. To Linsey's surprise and dismay he had accepted him immediately and, after only a few short days, seemed reluctant to let him out of his sight.

Jarvis appeared just as interested, if in a more detached way. He was leaving most of the initiative to Sean and Sean was responding beautifully. Jarvis was too clever to try and force their relationship too quickly and Linsey could see his restraint was paying dividends. It wouldn't be long now before Sean was practically eating out of his hand! With a twinge of bitterness she wondered if all the love she had expended on Sean counted for anything. Sometimes she felt betrayed, when she saw them together, and found it difficult to conceal her hurt.

That Jarvis was delighted with his son was obvious. He appreciated Sean's sharp intelligence and was already making plans for him. From Linsey he had demanded details of the boy's progress from birth. He wanted to know everything. Fortunately Linsey's answers hadn't aroused too many adverse comments. Although he didn't exactly praise her, she felt he had some approval for the way Sean had been brought up.

Up to a point, he said, she had done well, but from now on he took over. He didn't accuse her again of concealing his son from him, but he left her in no doubt that Sean's future lay in his hands. As Sean was his heir this was only to be expected, but she didn't like the way in which he brushed her opinions aside. He never consulted her about anything and, even if he condescended to listen, he rarely followed her advice.

She was thinking unhappily of this when Mark Lanier arrived and watched him approach with dismay in her eyes. She had forgotten she had promised to visit the plantation, and she felt guilty. Not that she had anything to feel guilty about, she assured herself hastily, but the Laniers had been good friends. She would have liked to have seen Mrs Lanier especially before she left, but she had been so busy packing for their departure tomorrow, it had quite slipped her mind.

'Hello,' Mark said huskily, his eyes resting on Linsey's lovely face hungrily, 'I came to see what was keeping you. I've looked for you every day. I would have come sooner, but I didn't know if I'd be welcome.'

'I'm sorry, Mark,' she apologised, with an uncertain smile. Sean was playing some distance away and hadn't noticed they had a visitor. Nervously she asked Mark if he wouldn't sit down. Then she tried awkwardly to explain what had happened—at least some of it. She felt forced to leave so much out that she couldn't blame Mark for being indignant.

'I don't believe it, Linsey!' he exclaimed, his good-looking face flushed with anger. 'You can't really mean to go back to him?'

'I have to, for Sean's sake. Don't you see?' Her voice rose, but her eyes, fixed on him, pleaded for understanding.

'Linsey?' She jumped to hear Jarvis's cynical tones behind her. What had he overheard—how much? As she turned from Mark, her face was full of unconscious apprehension.

'I didn't expect you back so soon, Jarvis.'

He shrugged, his eyes going narrowly to Mark. 'Aren't you going to introduce me to your friend?'

Trying to regain her composure, she did so. The two men nodded an acknowledgement of each other, but made no attempt to shake hands. Mark, viewing Jarvis bleakly, seemed suddenly at a loss for words.

Jarvis said smoothly, 'You must forgive me, but I haven't had time to meet many of Linsey's acquaintances. And as we're leaving tomorrow, it's not something I can easily redress.'

'Leaving tomorrow?' Mark swung on Linsey, his face white, unable to hide his dismay.

'Yes.' She went pale.

Mark clenched his hands, his jaw set. 'I'd like a few minutes alone with you, Linsey.'

'I'm afraid that isn't possible,' Jarvis broke in coldly.

'I would like to say goodbye to Mark's mother, though,' Linsey was surprised to hear herself saying quickly. She wasn't sure if she wanted to talk to Mark privately, but she felt she ought to see Mrs Lanier. Harriet would have expected it of her.

Mark sighed. 'Mother is giving a party this evening, Linsey. That's really what I called to see you about. She sent an invitation. Naturally,' he added stiffly, 'she would want this to include your husband, if he cares to accept.'

Linsey, waiting resignedly for Jarvis's refusal, was startled when he nodded suavely. 'Why not? If your mother has been Linsey's friend, Mr Lanier, I certainly mustn't miss this chance to thank her.'

CHAPTER SEVEN

SHORTLY after eight that evening, Linsey left with Jarvis to go to the party. Any enthusiasm she might have felt had waned during the past hours. The atmosphere in the car was strained. She was aware that Jarvis wasn't impressed with the dress she was wearing. He had said what he thought of it in no uncertain terms.

Staring at her closely, he had noted the ill fit of it, assessing, she had seen, the cheapness of the material. 'I presume you made it yourself?' he asked, 'like the one you wore on the yacht.'

'What if I did?' She glared at him, not wishing at that particular moment to be reminded of the yacht.

'After I took that off I should have dropped it overboard,' he taunted.

She flushed, but he had no pity for her. 'Doesn't Lanier notice what you have on when he takes you out, or does he never get past that low neckline?'

Protectively Linsey's hands had covered the deep cleavage. 'It was a mistake I couldn't rectify.' Sean had interrupted her concentration and she had made a mistake with the pattern. 'I'll wear a brooch.'

'Which might only attract more attention to your undoubted assets,' he murmured dryly. 'Better to leave it.

'I suppose you've had a very good social life since you came to live here?' he remarked, as they headed towards the Lanier plantation.

'Not really,' she replied, having had very little social life at all but reluctant to admit it. Nor, for some reason she was unable to understand, did she want him to believe she had been very gregarious.

'Looking after Sean couldn't absorb all your time?'

'You expect it to take all Miss Smith's,' Linsey said resentfully. 'Sean doesn't need her, Jarvis.'

'You mean you don't? She makes you feel insecure and you don't like it. You're not thinking of Sean at all.'

Because she suspected this might at least be partly true, she bit back a sharp retort. 'You can't blame me for beginning to wonder what I'm going to do with myself!'

'You'll have time for other things.'

He didn't explain what and somehow she hadn't the courage to ask him. 'I suppose so,' she agreed.

They came to a road junction and he slowed down, asking for directions. After Linsey gave them and he had taken the turning to the right, he glanced at her briefly. 'You aren't really upset about Miss Smith, are you, Linsey?'

She felt stunned that he should trouble to ask. 'I don't think so,' she hesitated, 'but, apart from anything else, Sean's an absolute bundle of energy and Miss Smith sounds too old for him. He could wear her out.'

'She's only in her forties, and looks as if she could cope with a dozen more like him,' Jarvis assured her dryly. 'I was lucky to get her at a moment's notice. If it hadn't been for an unfortunate cancellation I shouldn't have done.'

Linsey still didn't feel too enthusiastic. It might be all very well to be lazy on the yacht, and clearly Jarvis had decided she was to have little to do, but what about when they arrived in London? She knew all about nannies! Hadn't Harriet been one? They took over completely, in more ways than one—a mere mother didn't stand a chance! Arguing with Jarvis, though, could be like battering one's head against a stone wall. It might be wiser to drop the subject for a while, until she saw how things went.

Deliberately she turned her thoughts to the party they were on their way to attend. Why had Jarvis been so willing to go? In London he had always refused to accept casual invitations. For a moment, on the beach, he had looked positively hostile, then suddenly, unbelievably had turned into a cordial, if not over-effusive host. Linsey had noticed that Mark, despite his obvious distrust of her husband, had been impressed. By the time he left he appeared to have a grudging respect for Jarvis, which hadn't altogether surprised her. She had seen Jarvis at work in London. He could charm the birds off trees, as her mother used to say, if he felt like it.

As they neared the house, Jarvis warned, 'Please remember this evening, Linsey, that you're my wife. Unless you want to cause a lot of idle speculation you shouldn't forget it.'

'You don't have to worry.' She lowered her fair head. As they were leaving the island, she couldn't see that it mattered if she did give the gossips something to talk about. She wouldn't, of course, because she wasn't that kind of person, and it hurt that Jarvis should think she was.

'Good.' He drew up on the wide sweep of gravel at the end of the driveway. Coming around to her side of the car, he helped her out. With his hand under her elbow, he raised his head to look about him. 'These old houses are impressive,' he commented.

'I think so.' Standing by his side, she followed the direction of his wandering gaze with appreciation. The old Colonial style house before them was built on the lines of a French chateau and very striking. Yet, for all its size, it was a gracious house, full of warmth and charm and space.

'It must be a nice place to live,' Linsey didn't realise her voice was wistful.

'Does Lanier know you think so?' Jarvis asked coldly.

'No,' she replied, in a rush of confused embarrassment as Mark hurried from the house to meet them. 'How could he? It's not as if I'm free.'

With some misgivings, she saw it was a large party and wished she didn't feel so tired. She would rather it had been one of Mrs Lanier's smaller gatherings, with fewer people. Jarvis wouldn't mind, of course. Crowds had never worried him.

Mark escorted them to his mother. If his mother was curious over Jarvis's appearance she made no comment, but Linsey avoided being alone with her. She hoped Mrs Lanier wouldn't insist on a lot of unnecessary explanations. Harriet and Mrs Lanier in the past had often tried to throw Mark and Linsey together, but Linsey knew she wouldn't be back, not even after she was divorced. Mark meant nothing to her and never would.

She found herself having to tell Mark this later, as they danced together and he began begging her to return. It hurt her to have to refuse. 'It's better to be honest, Mark,' her blue eyes darkened with distress as his face went white. 'You wouldn't want me to pretend?'

An hour later, Jarvis struggled through the crowd of young men surrounding her to ask her to dance. She hadn't seen Mark for quite a while. He had hinted that he might go and get drunk.

Jarvis, pulling her closer than was necessary, said, 'Perhaps I should make sure all those young hopefuls who've been swarming round you know you aren't available?'

Linsey, trying to put a little space between them, wasn't paying much attention. 'They're simply friends, some not even that.'

'Some would like to be more, especially Mark

Lanier.'

'Well, you don't want me.' She tried to keep her voice light.

'You never know,' he glanced down at her contemplatively. 'You're still very delectable, Linsey,' his eyes lingered on the soft swell of her breasts, 'You're probably more attractive now than when I first knew you.'

Her heart missed a beat and she wished the neck of her dress had been higher. Sharply he pulled the lower half of her body against his hard thighs until she was aware of every part of him. Her heart pounding, she drew a deep breath, terrified of the crazy way her senses were responding.

'You can still arouse me,' he muttered thickly, his mouth against her cheek, his hand gripping closely on her narrow waist, 'but then you must have known that last week.'

'Jarvis!' she protested, as he held her even tighter and she felt his body hardening with desire moving sensuously against her own. Her face began to burn. He must be deliberately teasing her, for while his voice was warm, a quick glance perceived that his eyes were cold.

What kind of a man was he? To her relief he let her ease away from him, making no comment on her flushed cheeks. Afterwards he appeared quite content to stand aside and watch her dance with other men again. Even when Mark returned to claim her, he didn't seem to mind. She believed he was enjoying himself, but just after midnight, when she pleaded a headache, he had no objection to taking her home.

'I don't like leaving Sean too long, either,' she told him, after they had said goodbye to their hosts and were in the car. 'Musetta is very good, but I worry.'

'Two of my best men from the yacht are also keeping an eye on him,' Jarvis reminded her dryly.

'He's used to me, though,' she said stiffly. 'I'm glad I'm going with him tomorrow.'

'You don't have to do anything for his sake, you know. That might be a mistake,' he said curtly.

Linsey started. Sitting up straighter in her seat, she stared at him accusingly. 'So you did hear Mark and me talking on the beach?'

'It wasn't difficult.'

She frowned, bewildered. 'You obviously didn't care for the conversation, so why did you accept Mark's invitation?'

Jarvis glanced at her cynically. 'I decided it might be a good chance to discover the extent of your—er—romantic involvement, if you like.'

'And—your conclusions?' Because she didn't really want to know them, she hoped he wouldn't reply.

He had no intention of sparing her, however. 'You could be having an affair with him, but he really leaves you cold, doesn't he?'

'Yes.' A long time afterwards, Linsey was still regretting being foolish enough to say that. 'I've never had an affair with him, though, whatever you may think,' she added fiercely. 'He asked me to marry him.'

'Bloody cheek!' Jarvis snapped, only that, nothing more, but he drove the rest of the way home quite savagely.

The next morning they locked up the house for the last time. They had arranged to leave the keys with Harriet's solicitor whom, unknown to Linsey, Jarvis had been in touch with.

Linsey had said goodbye to the Laniers and her friends in the village; now there was only Musetta. She had felt sad about leaving the others, but she found herself weeping a little over Musetta. The two girls, one pale and delicate-looking, the other darker, clung together with wet cheeks. Musetta was getting married and was very happy, but she vowed she would never forget Linsey and Sean. Jarvis had to almost prise them apart, and, as he did so, he pressed an envelope containing quite a large sum of money into Musetta's hands. It was a wedding present, he said. And because he was grateful to her for looking after his wife and son he had added a little extra.

Musetta, overwhelmed, wept again as she saw them off. 'Quite a touching occasion,' Jarvis said dryly.

'It was good of you to be so generous,' Linsey sighed. 'I bought her a small present, but I hadn't anything of real value to give her.'

'I expect she'll treasure your present long after my money is spent.'

'Perhaps.' She was surprised at his sensitivity.

The journey to the yacht was more nostalgic than she had thought it would be. During the week Jarvis had stayed with them she had shown him something of the island. It had been easier, she had discovered, than spending too much time on the beach where the sight of his lithe body, clad only in black swimming trunks or a pair of faded cotton shorts, disturbed her too much. When he had suggested, one day, that they might take Sean out, she had agreed eagerly. Too eagerly, she suspected, as the knowing look in his eye hinted that he was not unaware of her reasons.

Sean had enjoyed exploring Mauritius and so had she. From the sleepy little fishing villages in the south they had driven up to Plaine Champagne, the highest part of the central plateau, with its superb view of the Black River Gorges, and after that they had had lunch at one of the island's many hotels. During the afternoon they continued until they had almost circled the whole island. Sean had slept on the way home.

'Why hasn't he seen these places before now?' Jarvis had asked.

'Harriet didn't like going far, and you forget we

didn't have a car. This is only the second time I've been around the island myself.'

'You didn't take Sean?'

'Sean was only a baby,' she explained. 'I wasn't there with another man, if that's what you mean. Mrs Lanier and Harriet were going to visit a mutual friend and asked me to go with them.'

'Why did you call him Sean?'

The abruptness of his query dismayed Linsey, although it wasn't entirely unexpected. She had known he didn't like the name, but when he hadn't mentioned it again she had decided he was prepared to accept it.

'I'm not sure,' she confessed. 'Harriet liked it.'

'I might have guessed.' He glanced at her grimly. 'You didn't think of calling him after me?'

She turned her head too quickly to meet the cool censure in his eyes. 'I did—but . . .'

'You didn't want a constant reminder?' he finished the sentence for her, as she hesitated.

'Probably not.' When his mouth tightened angrily, she stammered in hasty confusion. 'One day, when you marry again, you can have more sons . . .'

He hadn't denied this, but his eyes had narrowed as he asked. 'Would you like more children?'

'I should have done. A big family must be nice,' she had sighed, thinking that if she had had a brother or sister she mightn't have been so lonely now. 'But you don't have to worry about that.'

She could have bitten her tongue out when he retorted mockingly, 'It's not something you can manage on your own.'

Colour had tinted her skin deeply and she had been relieved to see they were back at the house. Merely by talking this way, Jarvis could make her pulse race, and she was sure he often did it deliberately.

The yacht delighted Sean. She was certain, during the next few days, he must have explored every bit of it several times over, but in the company of the indefatigable Miss Smith he came to no harm. Miss Smith was quite an acquisition, Linsey had to admit. She was friendly and efficient, well able to keep Sean occupied for the greater part of each day, so that Linsey saw very little of him. Sean, for his part, appeared to find Miss Smith a satisfactory if younger edition of Harriet and had no complaints. Sometimes Linsey wished he had, for she still resented that he was so pleased with the new turn his life had taken. She had to remind herself that at his age he was too young to assess things very deeply.

Sean's frequent absence meant she was alone a lot with Jarvis. Whether Jarvis deliberately planned this or not, she didn't know. When she lay on deck, in the sun, beside the pool, he often joined her, but usually he kept his distance. He did nothing to frighten her by being over-friendly, although occasionally she caught him scrutinising her bikini-clad form closely. When she arrived on the yacht she found he had provided her with a wardrobe of new clothes, among them half a dozen bikinis. A white one was her favourite, but she still felt selfconscious in it as it barely covered her.

She was wearing it one afternoon a few days later. Jarvis was stretched out beside her. They had just finished lunch and Linsey was drowsy with good food and the heat. Miss Smith had settled Sean for his siesta and was in the saloon writing letters.

The yacht was quiet, there was no one about. Linsey slid a quick glance at Jarvis. His long, powerful body was bare, apart from the brief, shabby shorts he often went around in. His eyes were closed, his thick lashes heavy on his cheeks, his well shaped mouth relaxed and sensuous. He had a strong face. Her breath caught strangely as she studied it. It seemed a long time, years, since she had watched him like this as he slept.

Once she had awoken early, in the first week of their

marriage, and had a crazy desire, she remembered, to trace her mouth over his face. She hadn't, of course. She hadn't been able to find the right kind of courage. She wondered if she could have done it now, supposing the situation had been different. She knew she wasn't quite so young any more, but although she had changed she wasn't sure that she had lost all her old inhibitions.

Jarvis opened his eyes and caught her staring at him. His mouth quirked a question. 'So?'

Colouring, she reached quickly for the coffee the steward had left. 'It's getting cold. Do you want any? I wasn't sure whether to wake you or not.'

'Is it only the coffee that's cold?' he murmured drowsily.

To her consternation, he lifted a hand, stroking it lazily across her bare midriff. Beneath his taunting fingers her skin tingled. She drew a sharp breath.

His hand, on her indrawn breath, tightened. He said softly, 'I still make you jump?'

'The unexpected can make most of us do that.'

'But the first shock must be over now, so why don't you breathe normally?'

She glared at him, trying to. She wished he would take his hand away. It probed, as if he was playing a piano, slowly and thoughtfully. By contrast, sensation from his fingers was piercing her swiftly. Her breathing continued to be uneven.

'You're so slender,' his voice came softly as his hand stretched an octave to span her waist. 'No one would believe you'd ever had a son. How did you look when you were carrying Sean?'

If she had flinched from his touch, she positively recoiled from his query. Yet what could be more telling than refusing to answer? 'The same as other girls, I suppose, in that condition. Not too attractive.'

'Did you believe yourself to be unattractive?'

She could feel his eyes boring into her, but refused to look at him. It had been a time of bitterness, which should have been all happiness, but she couldn't expect any sympathy from Jarvis on that score. It hadn't taken her long to realise what she was missing was an adoring husband, who would only view her increasing size with approbation and protective love. She had missed Jarvis and wanted him, but had been unable to bring herself to get in touch with him.

'I—I felt unattractive,' she said at last.

Carefully he removed his hand from her waist. 'I should have liked to have seen you.'

A lovely warmth flooded her. Quickly she lifted her head. Was he trying to tell her something? She was disappointed that his expressionless gaze told her nothing. He could have meant anything. His green eyes gave no clue. If anything, they made her shiver.

She swallowed, knowing she was being silly to imagine he hated her. Jarvis had never felt that strongly about anyone. 'You were spared that, at least.' She was determined to be flippant.

'As you say,' he shrugged.

He was avoiding direct answers, and unhappily Linsey wondered why. She wondered, too, why he had touched her so intimately. His mood had varied since they had sailed from Mauritius. As long as she didn't actively oppose any decision he made regarding Sean, he was coolly friendly.

He shot her another look, as though measuring the degree of her uncertainty. Despite the casual tone she adopted, her small face was flushed, her eyes bewildered. 'I'll have that coffee, if you don't mind. If you can be bothered to pour it out?'

'Yes, of course.' She flinched from the hint of criticism in his voice. Her hand shaking with childish indignation, she grabbed the coffee pot. 'You sound as if you think I'm growing lazy!'

As he accepted a cup of lukewarm coffee, his brow quirked sardonically. 'If you are, then laziness suits you. You look quite blooming, so I shouldn't complain. I imagine this was how you looked before you had Sean.'

'Before . . .?' She frowned. She had been absorbed in the long, clean lines of his body and only half aware of what he was saying. 'Oh, you mean . . .?'

'How bright you are today!' he smiled. 'But skip the question. It doesn't matter.'

Linsey felt she was on a rack. Why was he baiting her about Sean, for this, she was sure, was what he was doing? Life on board ship could be boring. She didn't find it so, but if Jarvis did he could be amusing himself at her expense to pass the time.

Feeling an urge to escape him, she dived into the pool, but he watched, with that oddly calculating look she was beginning to dread. It was beginning to frighten her, because she didn't know what it meant. She could guess, but she had never been much good at guessing where Jarvis was concerned. If he was trying to punish her a little for leaving him, he was certainly succeeding.

She tried floating on her back, but his eyes followed, scorching her. She was impatient with herself for allowing him to distract her, but the pool was no longer a sanctuary. Swiftly, but with clumsy strokes, she swam to the other side and climbed out.

Water dripped off her long, slender limbs and she was disconcerted to find her bikini top had slipped. As she pulled it back in position, her heart flipped as she realised Jarvis was still studying her over the rim of his coffee cup. She went pink and a strange shudder shook her. He never missed a thing!

Thinking she must be cold, she turned to find her towelling robe which lay at the other side of him. As she approached, he caught hold of her ankle. His hand, as it curved the fine bone, was just as sensuous as it had been on her waist.

'Are you going to your cabin?' he asked.

'Yes.'

'I'll join you,' he smiled lazily.

Was this a suggestion? Jarvis had a clever way with words. He never committed himself, not if he could help it. They had separate cabins. The last thing she wanted was him in the one she occupied.

'Why?' She forced a cool little smile, tossing the ball back in his court with what she hoped was some degree of sophistication.

Letting go of her ankle, he came to his feet, like a cat, towering above her. Putting a hand on her arm, as if to help his balance, he murmured, 'The owner of any property has the right to inspect it occasionally.'

Was he speaking of her cabin? He hadn't been there since he had shown her to it, before they sailed. She could still feel the touch on her ankle and waist. She wished he would let go of her arm, it was somehow affecting her thinking.

'I'm sure your steward would report if anything was wrong.'

'I might ask him to report how you look first thing in the morning. I might even try bringing in your tea myself. There's nothing like learning first-hand.'

Linsey, very conscious of colour stealing into her face, glared at him. 'I don't want you in my cabin, Jarvis. That wasn't part of the arrangement. I didn't agree . . .'

'Because there was no definite arrangement,' he snapped. 'I invited you to come along, if you liked. You said you would. I advised you to sleep on it, which you did. Next morning you hadn't changed your mind, but there was nothing drawn up. We agreed on one or two things, but only in the widest terms.'

'You didn't insist on anything in writing!'

'Without a lawyer,' he retorted curtly, 'it wouldn't have been worth the paper it was written on.'

'I could have seen Harriet's solicitor.'

'You could have,' he looked irritated, 'but you knew as well as I did, you didn't have a leg to stand on regarding Sean. You still don't. You're looking for a stronger case before you get that far.'

Was she? Linsey wished she knew. She wasn't sure any more what she did want. There didn't seem a clear-cut thought in her head, these days. Fretfully she glanced up to meet the derisive stare of hard green eyes. Her sigh was one of submission and he took it as such.

'So,' he said dryly, 'I can come to your cabin? No more arguments?'

Numbly she shook her head.

Jarvis relented a little at her abject expression. 'I merely wish to talk about something, without the risk of interruption. If you go ahead, I'll be with you in a few moments.'

Rather than provoke another quarrel, she nodded. She must have been crazy to imagine he would want to do anything else but talk.

In her cabin she showered but didn't have time to dress before she heard his arrival. Hastily towelling her long fair hair, she combed it. It would have to do as it was, there was no time to dry it properly and pin it back. Instead of dressing, she reached for another robe, a longer one, thinking it covered her better. She didn't notice how the thin silk clung to and emphasised her every curve.

When she came out of the bathroom, Jarvis was lounging on her bed, his hands behind his head. It reminded her so vividly of the last time they had been together like this that she turned, diving towards her wardrobe.

'If you wait, I'll get dressed,' she exclaimed, in a

shaken voice.

He was off the bed in a trice, pulling her round to him as she fumbled with the wardrobe door. 'You don't have to, I won't stay long.' The line of his mouth suddenly taut, he stared down at her. 'Come and sit down. You look beautiful as you are, and I'm sure I can keep my hands off you for five minutes.'

He had changed into a pair of casual pants and slung a shirt around his broad shoulders. The shirt he had left unbuttoned. It was a hot day and heat seemed to be dancing off his bare body. She wondered if he had any idea what he was doing to her.

Jerking from him, she made to sit in a chair, but he caught hold of her again and drew her down beside him on the bed.

'Sit there and prove you can resist me for a similar length of time.'

'What is this?' she asked coldly. 'Some sort of game you're playing? Did you really want to see me about something, Jarvis, or are you merely trying to amuse yourself?'

He glanced at her cynically as she sat stiffly erect, away from him. 'You stopped amusing me a long time ago, Linsey,' he said cryptically. 'No, I wanted to tell you that I'm sending Sean and Miss Smith home from Spain. I'm picking friends up there. At this stage, I think he'll be better out of the way. Besides, his cabin and others will be needed.'

Linsey flickered a quick look at him, her pulses jumping nervously. 'It's your boat, of course, and your friends, but couldn't you have done without them for once? You said you wanted to know your son. Now you're sending him away.'

'The arrangements were already made, before I knew I had a son,' he replied curtly. 'I dropped these people off. They have a villa in Spain, and I arranged to pick them up. I had no means of knowing I was going to find other company.'

Linsey flushed at the cool rebuke in his voice. It was she who was being unreasonable. 'I'm sorry,' she apologised, 'I wasn't thinking. I'd rather go with Sean and Miss Smith, though, if you don't mind.'

'I do mind,' he said firmly. 'You're still my wife and you stay with me. People will think it odd if you disappear again.'

She hadn't thought of this. 'Would anyone remember me?'

'I'd be surprised if they didn't,' his voice was dry, 'there was too much of a stir when you disappeared for them to forget. One of the things I'm going to enjoy most about our so-called reunion is the reaction of those who, as I said, secretly believe I did away with you.'

She glanced at him quickly, but his face was so grim she changed her mind about making a joke of his remark. If anything she felt a fresh wave of shame. It was something that had never occurred to her, but it couldn't have been pleasant for Jarvis, to be suspected of some terrible crime.

Linsey felt it inadequate but said, 'At least that's something I can put right.'

He made no reply.

She tried again, reverting to Sean. 'Won't he be frightened when he arrives in London? It's not as if he had been there before. He won't know anybody.'

'My mother will meet him. He and Miss Smith will stay with her. Later we'll take him to the country. He should enjoy living at Worton. Don't you agree?'

'Who wouldn't?'

'I'm glad you appreciate something,' his expression was veiled. 'Neither of you will have as much freedom as you had on Mauritius, though. You understand that?'

Linsey wasn't sure she did. There was a hint of

hidden threat in his voice that she didn't like. 'The kind of life we led on Mauritius is fine, but it gets a bit pointless after a time. I don't really appreciate limitless freedom, nor do I like being idle.'

'Well, there won't be a lot to do at Worton,' he looked at her thoughtfully. 'In normal circumstances, we might have enlarged our family, which would have kept you busy and given you something to think about.'

Colour flooded Linsey's face and she lowered her head to hide it from him. 'I'll probably train for something,' she took a deep breath to try and stop her heart beating so fast, 'then I'll be able to keep myself after our divorce.'

Again he didn't reply. It might have been better to leave it, but something compelled her to ask. 'You do want a divorce, don't you?'

'I'm not so sure,' he drawled, startling her, so her eyes swung to him involuntarily, widening. 'A wife can be useful, in more ways than one.'

'But I thought you wanted to remarry.'

'I'm in no hurry.'

Linsey felt pain moving within her, sharpening in her throat. She knew her eyes must reflect some of it, yet she couldn't remove them from his face. 'Is your friend willing to wait?'

'Women always are, I've found, but I think we've already discussed this.' He paused, the light contempt in his voice fading. 'How about it, Linsey? It will be easier living together if we can be friends.'

Thoughts sped like lightning through Linsey's head as she glanced away from him. It mightn't be so easy, living with Jarvis on this basis. She might have managed if he continually ignored her and treated her as an enemy, but friendship was another thing. It was neither one thing nor another and might simply become a torment. She might look much the same as she had done when she was eighteen, but underneath she was different. She wasn't sure how she felt about Jarvis any more. Her feelings seemed different, more intense. Before, they had consisted of a lot of yearning, of excitement, of wanting him but holding back. Now, despite her efforts to ignore it, everything about him affected her deeply. Her emotions resembled an unplumbed well. If she didn't watch out she might drown in them. It had begun in his cabin, the first time he had brought her to the yacht, the feeling of being swept away. She didn't want this to happen again. Yet, at the same time, what he was asking wasn't unreasonable, and, if she didn't want to lose Sean, what could she do but agree?

'If I go to Worton,' she said slowly, 'and you're living in London, I'm sure it shouldn't be all that difficult to be civil to each other.'

'Because you think we'll rarely meet?' His mouth thinned impatiently. 'I'll be home each evening, Linsey. Some days I won't even be going anywhere, and some weeks I'll want you in London with me.'

'Why?'

'I entertain a lot. I need a hostess. You were shaping very nicely before you went away.'

Only that? Nervously she bit her lip. 'What if I refuse?'

Steadily Jarvis stared at her. 'Refuse if you like,' he replied, almost indifferently, 'but first make sure you really want to.'

CHAPTER EIGHT

SUDDENLY Linsey knew she wasn't going to refuse. More than anything else she wanted to go to Worton with Sean and Jarvis. She wasn't sure what she was committing herself to, but nothing could surely be worse than a lifetime without them.

'Be very sure,' Jarvis repeated his warning, 'that you don't love another man. I know you don't love me, but once you agree to come to Worton I might not be in a hurry to let you go again.'

She said, 'There isn't anyone else, and I've nothing else to do.'

His eyes narrowed. Again, for a split second, Linsey thought she saw hate in them. 'I just imagine it,' she whispered.

'What was that?' He glanced at her sharply.

'Nothing,' guiltily she shook her head. 'I was talking to myself.'

'A bad habit.' His eyes lingered suspiciously, then, to her surprise, he smiled.

When he smiled at her like that, like a cat taunting a canary, he made her shiver. At the same time she felt feverish and different. Here in the privacy of the cabin, she had a sudden desire to put her arms around him and prove she was different from the half-awakened girl she had been during the first weeks of their marriage.

She must be taking leave of her senses! As she shrank back with an audible gasp, the mockery in Jarvis's eyes deepened. He must have read her thoughts and was amused by them.

Coolly he rose to his feet and moved away. 'I have

work to do, I'm afraid. I'll see you later.'

'Jarvis?' she stammered, wanting to let him go yet having an insane desire to delay him. 'You haven't told me anything about these people you're picking up. Do I know them?'

'I shouldn't think so. They were abroad when you lived with me. Anthony and James Forsyth, two brothers, married, no children.'

'No,' she agreed as she met his eyes, 'I can't remember them.'

Jarvis lifted a hand in a sketchy salute, which nevertheless warned her to refrain from delaying him any longer. 'See you later,' he said again.

The few days it took them to reach the South of France passed pleasantly. Jarvis spent hours in his cabin working, but he also spent a lot of time with Sean and Linsey. They called occasionally at different resorts, of which there was quite a choice, scattered along the Italian and French coast. Often he took them ashore and sometimes, hours later, would send Sean back to the yacht with Miss Smith while he and Linsey dined somewhere. These excursions she began to enjoy very much, and she frequently found herself wishing that they didn't have to end. The long days afloat, during which the worries of the last months rapidly faded, renewed a lot of Linsey's old vitality. These days she laughed with Sean, instead of continually checking him nervously, and when Jarvis talked with her and argued, there was often a sparkling challenge in her eye and a colour to her cheeks which was altogether attractive. She was young and alive, her whole life before her, and was beginning to discover she liked it.

Jarvis was picking his friends up at Menton, but they arrived the day before, to take Sean and Miss Smith to Nice, a little farther along the coast, and see them off from Côte d'Azur Airport.

When this was accomplished, Linsey and Jarvis

returned to Menton and the yacht, to change and dine in one of the luxury hotels, set in a cool avenue of palms, sycamore and orange trees. Menton had a charm all of its own, Linsey thought. It was a bustling old town of small shops and delightful little cafés, and in every corner was a profusion of semi-tropical flowers and plants—the kind of place she could have spent hours just wandering around. Even the air seemed to resemble the wine she and Jarvis were drinking.

Linsey wore the white dress which Jarvis had bought her in Nice, after they left the airport. To cheer her up, he had said. It was a light, filmy material, sprinkled with glittering diamanté, and looked wonderful with her heavy, silvery-fair hair and startling blue eyes. There had been an odd look in Jarvis's eyes as he lifted the cubicle curtain to watch her try it on. When she swung round, startled, wondering how much he had seen, she had been uneasy at the dark red colour running under his skin. The saleswoman had simpered knowingly and Jarvis had turned abruptly away, leaving Linsey feeling she was the only one to be bewildered.

The meal Jarvis chose, without consulting her, was excellent, as was the coffee and the wine, and afterwards they danced on the terrace by the light of the moon to dreamy music. Linsey enjoyed it, but was aware that Sean's departure had depressed her. Underneath her assumed gaiety was a weight of anxiety. Would he be all right? Could he possibly manage without her? Jarvis had told him days ago that he was going to fly to London and he hadn't seemed to mind. If anything he had been excited and had asked a lot of questions about London and his new grandmother. It was only at the actual moment of leaving that he had clung apprehensively to Linsey.

'Daddy says I must keep a stiff—a stiff something,' he had whispered tearfully, as she kissed him goodbye.

'Upper lip, perhaps?' she whispered back, tears in her own eyes as he had valiantly nodded his small head. How could Jarvis expect so much of a three-year-old?

Thinking of it now, she sighed, and Jarvis asked if anything was wrong.

His arms were around her, they were scarcely moving to the music but she hadn't noticed. 'I can't help feeling worried about Sean.'

'You don't have to be worried,' he drawled. 'He's my son.'

Sean was, she realised resignedly. He had all his father's intellect and rationality, but he was so young. This was what Jarvis failed to understand. She glanced up at him anxiously. 'He's never been away from me before.'

'Then it's about time,' Jarvis said severely. 'You've been a mother now for over three years. Why not try concentrating on being a wife? It might make a nice change.'

Jarvis would only be fooling. 'It's not easy to forget him, to change, just like that.'

Jarvis said curtly, 'The role of a mother's been growing on you, to the exclusion of everything else. It's become a bad habit.'

'You can't call a child a bad habit!'

'Stop it, Linsey!' He pulled her closer as she strained indignantly away from him. 'You know what I mean. You aren't that dense!'

She was silent and he relented, but when she stumbled he sighed and took her back to their table. There he ordered champagne and insisted she shared it with him. They would drink to a new régime, he said curtly, or a relaxing of the old one.

Because his expression frightened her a little, she nodded, drinking recklessly. She tried to drown her growing uncertainty in the heady feeling imbued by the potent, expensive wine, and partly succeeded.

What did her fears amount to, really? A glimpse of
dislike in green eyes, a cold voice, a mouth which could
both hurt and charm. She had, Linsey told herself
severely, far too much imagination. Jarvis Parradine
was just an ordinary man and, more often than not,
men were frightened of women, rather than the other
way around.

Making a great effort, she tried laughing gently and
thought it had a good sound. It seemed to release
something gay inside her. Experimentally she drank
some more champagne and began talking of things that
didn't matter. Feeling better, she giggled. Jarvis
watched her wryly and smiled, then took her out on
the terrace where they danced again. This time she
didn't object to being held too closely.

When they got back to the boat she was still feeling
pleasantly adrift from the harsh world of reality. She
did have an uneasy suspicion that she wasn't walking
very straight, but she couldn't believe Jarvis would
have allowed her to drink too much.

'Goodnight,' she whispered, as the boat rocked,
causing her to clutch his arm to keep her balance. 'Is
there a storm brewing?' she asked.

His eyes glinted as he helped her down to her cabin.
'You could say.'

Inside, she staggered when he let go of her.
Everything seemed unreal. She felt unreal. She didn't
know what was happening to her.

He came into her cabin and closed the door. He
locked it with one hand, his other still holding her.
Then he looked down at her.

'Linsey?' The way he said her name made the blood
beat in her ears. When he whispered it again, still in
the same soft, thick voice, she raised a dizzy head to
stare at him in mute enquiry. It puzzled her that she
couldn't seem to see him properly. Anxiously she
wished she hadn't swallowed all that champagne.

Gently, when she didn't try to escape him, Jarvis lowered his mouth to trail it lightly over her flushed face, down the tip of her small, straight nose, until he reached her lips. He kept on being gentle until, instinctively, she tried to push him away. As if this angered him, he gathered her tightly to him. Holding her still, he crushed her mouth with his, parting her lips passionately.

It was such a sensual assault that she trembled. His kisses on her upturned mouth were ravishing, but somehow she didn't care. The fear which had always occupied a corner of her mind was gone. Not even when he began probing her mouth more deeply did it appear. Suddenly she was clinging to him with an aching sigh, pressing herself seductively to the hardening male contours of his body.

She could feel his heart beating loudly—or was it just the echo of her own? Drowsily she was aware of his hand stroking her back, the rounded curve of her hip and thighs, and a little sigh of pleasure escaped her.

'You like that?' he murmured thickly.

She nodded, liking the way he spoke to her, the dampness of his lips moving against her own. She was not too conscious of what he was doing to her, but she quivered beneath his probing hands, her arms going slowly around his neck. A feeling of pleasure was sweeping all over her and she wasn't trying to fight it. A pulse in her throat raced so fast she gasped and whimpered and could think of nothing but him. Jarvis's head was bent to the upturned curve of her breast and she buried her fingers tightly in his thick dark hair.

He didn't speak again, nor did she. It might have been that they both feared words might break these moments of fierce enchantment. Linsey had never surrendered completely to her emotions before. Always she had fought being totally overwhelmed by them.

Now she gave herself up to them, submitting to Jarvis's urgent demands with no thought in her head of holding back.

He was breathing heavily as he slid the narrow straps of her dress from her shoulders. Impatiently he dealt with zips and hooks. In his haste material tore, but neither of them heard it. Her head fell back over his arm as her dress fell to the floor and his hands came up over her rib-cage to caress her throbbing breasts. His mouth joined them, his tongue roughly teasing her distended nipples.

Linsey felt weightless as he lifted her, bearing her to the bed. He left her only long enough to strip off his own clothing, then he was lying beside her, her slim body crushed beneath the heaviness of his, the bareness of his skin bringing a burning tension to her own.

Dizzy excitement flooded her, drowning every sane thought. A searing longing soon had her writhing under him as his mouth sought and found her responsive lips before trailing a heated path over every inch of her. As their bodies slowly locked together, he muttered her name hoarsely, demanding and receiving total surrender. Her arms went around him as she wildly returned his passionate kisses, while, ruthlessly and with unerring precision, he possessed her completely.

When she woke next morning he was gone. Her hand went out, unconsciously seeking him, until she slowly came to realise he wasn't there. Then, as full recall followed almost instantly, she sat up, her cheeks flushed, immediately relieved that he wasn't still with her. She was grateful that she was alone, for having time to find an excuse for her shameless behaviour. Her face burned as she remembered how easily she had given in to his sensuous demands. Not only that. She had an awful suspicion that she had responded to him fiercely, with a hungry urgency she had never known before.

Jarvis was her husband. Last night he had also been an ardent and passionate lover, but that didn't mean that he loved her. With a hopeless sob, Linsey buried her hot face in her hands and wept.

Then, quickly, she tried to pull herself together. Leaving her bed, she showered and dressed, but only by condemning Jarvis's behaviour did she seem able to excuse her own. She stayed in the shower longer than usual, letting the water soothe her sore limbs, waiting for the old revulsion to come. When it didn't she was surprised, then confused, realising, for the first time, she had given herself completely, and without shame. Always, before, it had been there in the aftermath, making her feel soiled and sorry. This morning she felt neither, there was only a glorious feeling of well-being. It was as though some tight restriction which had been holding her was gone at last, leaving her wonderfully free.

Then she wondered what Sean was doing and was incredulous that she could have forgotten him. It had been hours since she had last thought of him. It didn't seem possible.

Flinging on some jeans and a tee-shirt, she ignored the dampness of her body and the tea which the steward had left while she was in the shower, and rushed out to find Jarvis. He would have been in touch with his mother by now and would know. She glanced in the saloon, but he wasn't there. Thinking he might be having breakfast, she went to the dining-room, only to be told that Mr Parradine was with the Captain.

'I'll have my breakfast after I speak to my husband,' she smiled radiantly at the steward, leaving him sighing with envy.

Jarvis was with the captain, but she didn't smile at him as happily as she had smiled at his steward. Some of the brightness in her face was missing as she blinked at him uncertainly.

After directing a somewhat confused good morning at both men, she turned to Jarvis. 'I've been looking for you to find out if Sean arrived safely. You'll have been in touch with London?'

Jarvis stared at her with a grimness she didn't immediately notice. 'Yes. I gather my mother met him and I believe he's settling in.'

'Oh, good!' Her relief was such that she grinned at the Captain, who had risen when she entered the cabin and was watching her intently. Linsey liked Carl Davis. He was a divorced man around Jarvis's age, and always very willing to talk to her. She didn't see Jarvis glance at them sharply. Linsey's fair, shining hair tumbled heavily about her shoulders, and her jeans and shirt clung to the slender lines of her figure. Because she hadn't spared the time to tie her hair back or dress properly, she looked young and beautiful but somewhat abandoned. That Captain Davis appreciated her extremely sexy appearance was more than apparent. He seemed to forget Jarvis was there. So did Linsey. For a moment she was curiously hypnotised by the Captain's intense regard.

Not so Jarvis. Almost roughly he took her arm, his fingers biting. 'Have you had breakfast?'

Her eyes returned to him, startled, registering a slight fear. 'No, not yet.'

'Well run along and get some. I'll join you for coffee later.'

Dismissed like a child! Obediently Linsey turned, her cheeks burning. Why didn't he treat her like a woman for a change? Why hadn't he put an arm round her and drawn her close? Carl Davis had been there, but that needn't have mattered. Unexpectedly tears stung her eyes. If Jarvis had cared two hoots, he would surely have given her some brief indication that last night had been as important to him as it was to her.

On her way to the dining saloon most of her bright confidence faded. Jarvis's harsh demeanour hurt more than she cared to admit, but she tried not to make too much of it. He might have had other things on his mind. Men often had and women tended to regard the smallest hint of indifference as a personal slight.

Nevertheless, he didn't join her for coffee and, after waiting around for a considerable time, she went back to her cabin. Somehow she didn't feel tempted to sun-bathe on deck this morning. She had been inclined to seek him out again, but she knew, if she did, she might not be able to find the courage to ask him the question uppermost in her mind. Why had he stayed with her throughout the night? She didn't remember sleeping much. Her heart accelerated when she recalled his lovemaking and beat even faster when she thought of her own response. Surely what had happened between them was going to make a difference? Jarvis's face, this morning, had been as hard as usual, but it didn't seem possible that he could treat her with the politeness of a stranger any more?

When he came to her cabin she was attempting to restore some order to her tangled hair. She was so startled to see him she almost dropped her hairbrush. 'Jarvis?' Despite her efforts to remain composed, a flush mounted her smooth cheeks. All her old ner-vousness returned, and it showed. Glancing at him quickly, she looked too quickly away from him again.

'The Forsyths will be here for lunch,' he told her briefly.

'Yes. I'll be ready.' She clutched the brush tightly, her hair falling all about her face. Her voice trembled, and she wondered what was wrong with her.

Jarvis snapped, 'You don't have to look at me like that, Linsey,' and, as her apprehensive gaze spun back to him, 'I don't intend to carry on where we left off last night, so you can relax.'

Now was her chance to say she wanted to, but she found she couldn't. She was angry with herself for reverting to the shy young girl she used to be, but his brusque tones shattered her nerves.

'D-didn't you enjoy—last night?' she faltered.

'What did it cost you to ask that?' he taunted. 'You were drunk and I took advantage of the state you were in. Maybe I wasn't quite sober myself. Oh, yes,' he continued remorselessly, 'I'll admit I enjoyed myself. You certainly know how to please a man when you've had too much champagne, but now you're stone cold sober, you can't even look at me, you're so embarrassed.'

'No,' anxiously she bit her lip, 'I don't think I am, Jarvis. Nor do I think I had all that much to drink, last night . . .'

'Words never convinced you, did they?' he mocked, 'but proof can be supplied in different ways.'

Before she could retreat he strode across the cabin and took hold of her. His hands hurt her shoulders as he jerked her to him. As her eyes widened apprehensively he grabbed a handful of her hair and pulled her head back, then he crushed her mouth savagely under his. It was a harsh kiss, she could feel the ruthlessness of his lips grinding the soft skin of her mouth against her teeth as though he hated her.

When he released her she swung up her hand, hitting him as hard as she could over his cheek. If he hated her, she returned his feeling exactly! A mist of white rage wavered in front of her and, if she could have managed it, she would have hit him again.

'Now do you understand?' he snapped coldly, and left her abruptly.

It was understandable that Linsey was late in getting ready to meet the Forsyths. She fumbled an awful lot, her fingers seeming all thumbs, and every now and again she had to cope with a strangled sob. Her brief temper had faded, but she felt more like collapsing on her bed than being pleasant to Jarvis's guests. As she applied make-up to her white face, the dark rings under her eyes, she hoped the Forsyths wouldn't be too observant.

When her cabin door opened again, the last person she expected to see was Jarvis.

Unsteadily she began, 'I didn't think I was all that late. I'll be ready in a minute. Are they here?'

'It doesn't matter,' he said curtly, surprising her. 'They were early. That wasn't what I came to see you about. The thing is, I've been speaking to my mother again and she isn't too happy about Sean.'

'Sean?' Linsey abandoned her lipstick, laying it down carefully, trying to combat a wave of alarm.

'It's nothing to get hot and bothered about,' he didn't give her a chance to ask what was wrong, 'Mother believes he might have caught a slight chill, but the line was bad.'

Linsey glared at him. 'I'm not getting hot and bothered, but surely it's normal to be anxious? Maybe you've not been a parent long enough to develop such instincts.'

His face went so hard and pale she shivered. 'Do I have to remind you that that's not my fault? Don't worry, Linsey, I'm quite as anxious as you are.'

'I'm sorry,' she whispered, 'I shouldn't have said that. I'll have to go to him, of course.'

'We'll both go,' he said firmly. 'I've already booked seats on an afternoon plane.'

'Oh, thank you!' Her heart felt immediately warmer that Jarvis should be willing to do this. She smiled at him. 'It's very good of you, Jarvis. I'm very grateful.'

'Hell, he's my son too, isn't he?' he snapped, his green eyes glittering with a kind of frustrated impatience.

'Of course,' she nodded, then suddenly frowned.

'But what about the Forsyths? What will you do about them?'

'They can still return on the yacht,' he shrugged. 'It has to come back, anyway. They won't mind, and it will give the crew something to do.'

'If I'd gone home yesterday,' Linsey fretted, 'Sean might have been all right and you wouldn't have needed to interrupt your holiday.'

'Do I have to keep reminding you that you're my wife and your place is with me?'

As she shrank from his icy blast, it took courage to form her reply. 'Ours isn't a normal marriage.'

'It never stood a chance.'

'Yes, that's true.' She was thinking of him and Olivia James.

'Well, just as long as the world believes there has been a beautiful reconciliation. No one need know it's only temporary. You can hate me as much as you like in private.'

Didn't he realise how much she loved him? 'I'd better pack a few things,' she said. 'I won't be long.'

'If you like,' he agreed, 'but don't pack too much. You can shop in London—and remember we have guests.'

Ten minutes later, when she followed him, she was stunned to find that Olivia James was one of the guests. Why hadn't Jarvis said something? He might have warned her! Feeling more like bursting into enraged tears, she was thankful no one noticed her approach. It gave her time to pull herself together.

Jarvis saw her first. Taking her arm, he drew her forward. 'You haven't met my wife,' he said smoothly, introducing her to the Forsyths. 'You remember Olivia, of course?' he added, without a change of tone.

Linsey nodded, unable to manage more than a polite smile, which was returned with a matching coolness. The Forsyths didn't appear to notice anything wrong.

'I'm sorry to hear about your son,' one of the wives murmured.

'I was so interested to hear about him,' Olivia interposed with acid sweetness. 'Does he happen to bear any resemblance to Jarvis?'

Her implication that Sean could be any man's son caused the Forsyths to stir with embarrassment. Not so Jarvis. 'Sean looks very like me,' he answered, when Linsey didn't reply.

Olivia laid a possessive hand on his arm. 'I can't wait to see for myself, darling. I'm coming to see him as soon as we reach London.'

Linsey's face went white and her eyes widened with a dismay she hadn't time to hide as she lifted them to Jarvis, but he merely said coldly, 'Olivia is travelling home with us.'

Linsey felt confused; nothing made sense. So this was the real reason Jarvis was returning to London? It wasn't because of Sean. He must simply be using Sean as an excuse to get himself to London and Linsey off the yacht. He wouldn't want to leave her on her own with the Forsyths, who might naturally ask her a lot of embarrassing questions.

'How nice for you—I mean, us, to have company,' she murmured, lowering her eyes from Jarvis's narrowed glance, hollowly proud of her coolness as she turned to begin talking to the Forsyths.

After lunch Jarvis had a few details to discuss with the Captain, and after he had gone the Forsyths decided to go down to their cabins and unpack. Linsey was left with Olivia, something she hadn't wanted to happen. Beside Olivia she felt as innocent as a newborn babe, but it wasn't a feeling which brought any satisfaction.

Olivia was a beautiful woman, tall and dark with a near-perfect figure. What assets she didn't have naturally, she had acquired in the course of her successful career. She seemed so at home on the yacht that Linsey could scarcely refrain from asking how many times she had been here before.

After asking the steward for more brandy, Olivia dismissed him. Coming to sit beside Linsey, she obliquely studied her glass.

'So you and Jarvis have got together again for a while?' she mused.

For a while? If Linsey had disliked Olivia's presumptuous way with the staff, she resented her remark more. Why did Olivia feel it necessary to ask such a question when it seemed she already knew the answer?

As Linsey clenched her hands tightly and regretted having refused a drink which might have sustained her, Olivia launched further into her attack.

'You must know that he intended divorcing you, but unfortunately he couldn't find you.'

Linsey wanted to get up and walk away, but something kept her frozen to her seat. 'He could have got a divorce any time, I believe, without my consent. If he really wanted one.'

'Oh, he did,' Olivia assured her quickly. 'He wanted to marry me. If it hadn't been for my career he would have made a greater effort to get a divorce.'

Why, Linsey wondered dully, if this was true, had Jarvis asked her to stay with him? It must be only for Sean's sake.

'Do you still want to marry him?' she decided to put it this way. It seemed less painful.

'Oh, yes,' Olivia's eyes glittered strangely, 'but not for another two years. I have my career to consider, but I'd like to marry before I'm thirty.'

'And—and have a family?'

'Not straight away,' Olivia shrugged. 'Jarvis and I haven't discussed it. We might make do with Sean. That is,' she finished vindictively, 'if this boy really is his son?'

It was then that Jarvis returned. A frown darkened

his face when he saw Linsey and Olivia were alone, but as he was followed almost immediately by the Forsyths he had no chance to say anything. The rest of the afternoon eventually passed and Jarvis didn't leave them again. Soon it was time to say goodbye, first to the Forsyths, who were still studying Linsey curiously, then the Captain.

The Captain had lunched with them but been called away before the meal was finished. He held Linsey's hand longer than necessary. 'I hope you'll find your son quite recovered, Linsey,' he said, his eyes devouring her.

Jarvis dragged her away, his fingers threatening to break her arm in two. 'Since when did you grant him that privilege?' he rasped in her ear.

She pretended not to understand. Carl Davis had used her Christian name before, but never when Jarvis was there. She didn't mind, in fact she liked it, but obviously Jarvis didn't.

The airport was busy and most of the empty seats on the plane were singles. Jarvis took the only double available, thrusting Linsey into the seat beside him. He had the air of a silently raging tiger, his height and size so intimidating, she hadn't the strength to defy him. Neither did Olivia, apparently. She was forced to take the seat across the aisle, which she did with extremely bad grace.

'I'm sure Linsey would rather sit here,' she turned to stare at Linsey, daring her not to offer.

Linsey had never met such hatred in anyone's eyes. 'I don't mind where I sit,' she agreed nervously.

'Well, I do,' Jarvis snapped. 'Stay right where you are.'

End of conversation, Linsey decided miserably, looking out of the window.

Leaning back in his seat, Jarvis lifted the armrest between them. 'You don't mind if I spread myself out a bit, do you? You're much smaller than I am.'

She shook her head, all too aware of the pressure of his shoulder, the muscles of his thighs pressing against hers. 'I don't mind,' she said.

Throughout the flight Olivia, who obviously regarded every setback as a challenge, chatted gaily to Jarvis. She talked animatedly about her next play and thanked Jarvis for backing her last one. Olivia's voice, when she liked to make it so, was husky and seductive. Linsey listened, with increasing unhappiness, as Olivia flirted openly with Jarvis.

Often Jarvis glanced at the small, still figure of his wife and asked if she was all right or if she wanted anything. Linsey merely nodded or shook her head. She tried not to be, but she knew she was jealous, desperately jealous of the intimacy which appeared to exist between the other two. It was making her so miserable she could have wept, but there seemed nothing she could do about it.

At Heathrow the air was cooler than in the South of France and Linsey shivered. Noticing it, Jarvis hustled her towards a taxi.

'Can we drop you?' this to Olivia.

Olivia, not to be disposed of so easily, tried a dazzling smile. 'I thought I'd ask your mother for a bed for the night. She's always so pleased to see me, darling.'

'Not tonight, Olivia,' Jarvis replied lightly but firmly.

He obviously didn't want his mistress and wife under the same roof. Scorn flickered in Linsey's violet blue eyes, but she lowered her lashes, hoping Jarvis hadn't seen it. She should perhaps be grateful for even this much consideration.

Olivia's regretful sigh was a long one. 'Then would you mind dropping me off at my flat?'

'Of course not.'

Linsey listened wearily to their conventional exchanges. Who did they think they were fooling?

He handed Olivia carefully into the taxi, then Linsey, then got in himself.

As the driver loudly banged in the gears and drove off, Linsey couldn't resist asking sweetly, under cover of the noise, 'Don't you want to sit in the middle, darling, beside her?'

Jarvis ignored this, which made her feel very young and foolish. As if to punish her, during the journey from the airport to the city, he talked to Olivia more warmly than he had done on the plane and ignored Linsey completely.

At Olivia's flat, Jarvis asked the taxi to wait while he saw her inside. When he returned there was a twist of triumph at the corner of his mouth. Quickly Linsey averted her eyes, feeling sick. Yet what, she asked herself, with a self-derisory shrug, could she expect? Jarvis was a man, a very normal one, as he had proved, and they had been apart for over four years. It would be ridiculous to assume that in all this time he had never looked at another woman. Olivia might not have been the only one, but it seemed significant that she was still around, especially as she was the reason why Linsey had left in the first place.

CHAPTER NINE

JARVIS'S mother also lived in a flat. Linsey wondered what Sean thought of it. Harriet's house had offered complete freedom and he had never known anything else. He had adapted very well to the restrictions of the yacht, but then he had been used to the sea all his life. His grandmother's flat, though large, was something else again, and Linsey felt doubtful.

She didn't express her fears to Jarvis, though, as he rang the bell and stood impatiently, waiting for admittance. Glancing at him anxiously, she remained silent by his side. When Sean recovered from his illness they would almost certainly be going to Worton. He would have plenty of room there.

'Do you still have the house in Chelsea?' she asked.

'Yes,' he replied, as the door opened, 'but we'll be going straight to Worton from here.'

A manservant let them in. 'Ah, Mr Parradine, sir,' he said, 'Mrs Parradine is expecting you.'

Jarvis's mother had been living in Paris with a cousin of Russian extraction at the time of their marriage. She had attended the wedding, but this was the last time Linsey had seen her. The cousin, an elderly lady, had since died and Mrs Parradine had returned to London. Linsey remembered her as a tall, regal-looking woman with the same faintly foreign accent which Jarvis also betrayed when he was angry about something.

Mrs Parradine was sitting in her magnificent drawing room, listening to a programme of classical music.

'Why, Jarvis!' she exclaimed, switching the radio off, 'how lovely to see you. And Linsey?' She paused, holding out her hands to the girl. 'I'm so pleased you're together again!'

Dutifully, Linsey placed her hands in the white ones held out to her, and kissed a delicately perfumed cheek.

'How's Sean?' she asked urgently, unable to contain herself a moment longer.

'Sean?' Mrs Parradine smiled. It was the first time Linsey recalled seeing her smile. Throughout the wedding ceremony she had frowned, and later Linsey had overheard her telling Jarvis his bride was beautiful but too young for him.

Now, when she spoke of her grandson, her face softened. 'He's a wonderful boy,' she exclaimed. 'So exactly like Jarvis was at that age. You were very naughty to run away and not tell us about him, Linsey. All these years we've missed.'

'Never mind about that now,' Jarvis, with a swift glance at Linsey's pale face, cut short his mother's gentle tirade, 'Linsey is worried about Sean. Perhaps we could go and see him.'

'But he's in bed asleep, my dears,' Mrs Parradine frowned on her son's tight-lipped appearance. 'The good Miss Smith has retired to her room, which adjoins his, and I'm sure she would have mentioned if anything was amiss. Last night,' her eyes were kinder as they rested on Linsey, 'Last night he cried for you, my dear, because everything was strange to him and he was missing you, but he hasn't been upset this evening. I went to see for myself, just half an hour ago, and he was sleeping like an angel.'

'But—I thought he was ill? You told me . . .' blankly Linsey turned to Jarvis.

'The line was bad,' he addressed his mother. 'You said he'd caught a chill?'

'Did I?' Bewildered, Mrs Parradine wrinkled her brow. 'I remember saying something about him feeling the cold, but that it might be the change of climate rather than a chill.'

'The line was very bad,' Jarvis repeated tersely.

'Was it?' His mother was obviously having difficulty remembering. 'Yes, perhaps it was. Anyway,' she brightened, 'I can assure you there's absolutely nothing wrong with him, he's very well indeed. Why don't you go and see him now, on your way to your room? You are staying, aren't you?'

'Only tonight,' Jarvis replied briefly, taking Linsey's arm.

'Go on, then,' Mrs Parradine smiled, 'see Sean and freshen up, then join me for dinner. I want to hear all about my new grandson!'

Apparently, on the rare occasions Jarvis stayed with his mother, he always occupied the same apartment. It was kept ready for him, and, after looking in on Sean, he took Linsey there.

Linsey was so relieved that Sean wasn't ill she scarcely realised where she was going. They had spoken to Miss Smith, who had repeated, almost word for word, what Mrs Parradine had told them. They had opened the door of Sean's room and seen him quietly sleeping. Linsey, recognising the glow of health on his face, knew she had worried unnecessarily.

As soon as the bedroom door closed behind them, however, she glanced around in dismay and exclaimed, 'I can't sleep here!'

'You don't have to wave a gun to frighten some women,' Jarvis jeered coldly. 'Just show them a double bed.'

'It's nothing to joke about,' she retorted tersely, trying to stay calm.

'No, it's not, is it?' he sighed grimly. 'Relax, there's a dressing-room. I'll sleep there.'

'Oh,' the racing beat of her heart slowed slightly, 'I see . . .'

'There's a lot you don't,' and he began flinging off his jacket.

His shirt had patches of sweat across the back and clung to his broad shoulders. Hastily Linsey looked away. 'I certainly don't understand why you pretended Sean was ill. You must have done it deliberately!' Discretion deserting her, she added, 'I suppose you couldn't wait to get back to London with Olivia?'

'Olivia?' His fingers paused on the buttons of his shirt, his face betraying nothing of his inner thoughts.

That Linsey's heart was nearly breaking, and it probably showed, did nothing for her composure. 'I know you're in love with each other and always have been, but you didn't have to go to such ridiculous lengths.'

'What the devil are you on about?' Yet he seemed to grasp the gist of her accusations, for his hand shot out cruelly to jerk her against him. When she gasped, like a fish out of water, his eyes went cold and hard. 'Listen, young woman. Yesterday, when we returned to the boat after seeing Sean and Miss Smith off, I instructed Davis to get in touch with London later, to confirm that they'd arrived safely. If they had, I told him I didn't want to know about it until morning.'

'Why not?' Linsey interrupted.

Jarvis frowned, studying her expression intently. 'I fancied,' he said silkily, 'it wouldn't do Davis any harm to imagine we were going to indulge in a night of erotic love.'

Heat coloured her pale cheeks, curling right down through her body. 'But we didn't!'

'We did,' he muttered thickly, his eyes on the trembling fullness of her mouth. 'What was left of it.'

'If we did,' she gasped, 'then you didn't enjoy it.'

'Who said I didn't?'

'You were full of disapproval this morning.'

'Only because you were so full of regret,' he snapped.

Thinking it better to get off such dangerous ground, she whispered, 'That doesn't explain what happened before lunch. All those alarming messages.'

'They weren't that alarming, surely?' he frowned. 'The first time I was merely relating what Davis had told me, which I might have explained if you hadn't annoyed me so.'

'Annoyed you?'

'If you'd been more decorously dressed and not enjoying quite so much the way Davis was staring at you.'

As if trying to clear her head, she shook it in bewilderment. 'I don't remember anything apart from being anxious about Sean.' And your unfriendliness, she almost added, but didn't.

A look of cold disbelief flashed over his face, but was as quickly concealed. 'We'd better deal with your suspicions first. After our row in your cabin, I decided to contact London myself and had just finished speaking to my mother when the Forsyths came on board with Olivia.'

'You weren't expecting her?'

'Of course not. Although,' he hesitated, 'I confess I wasn't too surprised.'

'You mean you thought she might come?'

'I thought nothing of the kind,' he snapped, his hands tightening on her shoulders, 'but I've had years of her turning up unexpectedly, years of trying to get rid of her. One has to use the most devious methods. Nothing obvious works with Olivia, her skin's too thick.'

Linsey hoped nothing was wrong with her hearing. She found it difficult to believe what Jarvis was telling her. 'If you didn't want her to come, why didn't you just order her off the yacht?'

'Perhaps because I've never learnt to be that ruthless,' he said tersely, 'and I know and like her family

But what I did today was as much to help the Forsyths as myself. It appears she turned up at their villa a few days ago and made a dead set at James.'

'I thought it was you,' Linsey faltered.

'And me,' he agreed dryly. 'Any man will do, come to that, but some of us she seems to like better than others. She's attractive, but the only thing she's in love with is her career. She's been divorced twice, but her marriages never stood a chance. When I saw her coming this morning, I knew I had to act fast, if I wanted to avoid days of chaos. I suppose I guessed, when I told them Sean had a chill, that she would decide to return to London with me, but it seemed I might be doing the Forsyths a good turn.'

Linsey didn't know how she felt, but it wasn't good. Was it possible she could have been wrong about a lot of things? 'Miss James told me after lunch that you were going to get married—after our divorce.'

'She said that?' Jarvis threw back his head incredulously.

Linsey stared at the strong brown line of his throat. 'You mean you aren't going to . . .?'

'No.'

Somehow Linsey found the nerve to ask, 'Haven't you ever been in love with her?'

'No,' he assured her sardonically, 'I have not. In fact,' his tone went grim again, as if he didn't particularly enjoy having to make such disclosures, 'I told her frankly, some weeks after we were married, that I wasn't prepared to put up with her making a nuisance of herself any longer. She was forever ringing up and calling at my office, whenever the whim took her. I had her weeping with remorse in my arms, promising to reform. Unfortunately she never gives up, not completely.'

'She said you backed her last play.'

'And you think that's given her fresh encouragement?' Jarvis's mouth twisted at Linsey's apparent lack of trust. 'The producer is a friend of mine, he asked me to back it. Olivia only had a minor part, although she's quite a good actress.'

Linsey stared at him and suddenly a torrent of words tumbled from her lips. 'She was the reason why I left you, why I ran away. I thought you were having an affair with her.'

Jarvis's face went pale with a cold rage. He looked like a man unable to believe the evidence of his own ears. 'You don't mean to tell me that you ran off to Mauritius just because of that? You thought I was having an affair, you didn't even wait to ask. You ended our marriage, caused me years of anxiety, because of what? An outsize imagination—or did you believe a pack of lies? Either way,' he ground out savagely, his eyes glittering, 'you deserve a thrashing, and if I was any kind of man at all, I'd give you one!'

He looked so furious Linsey feared he might and shrank away from him. Twisting from him, she stood panting against the dressing-table, feeling like death. Whatever had possessed her to make such a confession? The time hadn't been right, but she hadn't been able to stop herself. And how could she tell him the whole truth when he was staring at her with such hate in his eyes? He didn't love her, so there was no point in pouring her heart out.

'I'm sorry,' she whispered at last, through ashen lips.

'Sorry!' he snapped his teeth, a vicious sound. 'Do you know, the first time I saw you again, on Mauritius, I vowed I'd make you suffer, and by heaven I will! I'll employ no half measures, either. You talk of being sorry. One day soon you're going to know the true meaning of the word!'

'You—you didn't seem to want me,' Linsey began, tears streaming down her face.

'God!' he snapped, 'you can say that to a man only married a few weeks! You mean you didn't want me. I have my faults, but at least I tried to stick to my side of the marriage contract. I'd have had to shut myself away like a hermit to avoid other women completely, but I was never more than polite to any one of them—after I married you.'

Briefly Linsey closed her eyes in abject misery. What had she done? She seemed to be left without a single excuse for running away. Why hadn't she had the sense to think things out for herself instead of panicking like a schoolgirl? She couldn't even shelter under the guise of that any more, for her honeymoon with Jarvis, though short, had rapidly changed her into a woman. Or almost, she reminded herself, recalling with impatience now her crazy little hang-ups. It wouldn't have seemed so bad, perhaps, if she had let him know she was in Mauritius. She had been ill, but not so ill she hadn't known what she was doing.

'I—I'll try to make amends.' Even to her own ears this sounded futile.

'You really think that's possible?' Jarvis snarled.

The line of his jaw was concrete, the glitter in his eyes annihilating. He confused and terrified her so much she couldn't think. She was conscious that she had made a great mistake and must try and put it right somehow, but no immediate plan sprang to mind. Surely, in time, one would? There must be some way she could convince him she had changed and was full of remorse for what she had done.

'We—we mustn't keep your mother waiting,' she began unhappily, as he made no further attempt to break the tense silence. Desperately she hoped that Mrs Parradine's bracing company might help to clear her head and make Jarvis decide to be a little kinder. If they remained here much longer they might both say things they might regret. 'I'll just wash my hands,' she said. 'I won't be a minute.'

His face entirely unforgiving, Jarvis laughed. 'After we've been parted for so long she probably expects us to get delayed in our bedroom!'

Linsey's colour fled, there were only two bright, feverish spots of red on her cheeks. Was this the beginning of her punishment, a full measure of scornful taunts?

Later, when they returned to the bedroom, she was no nearer to finding a solution to her problems. She had thought of offering to give Sean up, but knew this would be impossible. And supposing she did make such a sacrifice, she was sure it wouldn't help her to regain Jarvis's love. Any hopes she had entertained in that direction had been sadly crushed by this evening's disclosures. A new idea occurred to her, one that made her flush painfully. Could she in any way compensate for her sins by offering to live with him as though theirs was a normal marriage? He didn't want a divorce, and she believed that while some men did stop loving their wives they still made love to them.

Linsey began restlessly unpacking the few clothes she had with her, scarcely aware of what she was doing. During dinner, despite his mother being there, Jarvis had been far from friendly. Nothing in his manner had suggested he would welcome such a proposal, yet how could they live together in a state of constant enmity? It wouldn't be easy to more or less offer herself to him, but being so much in the wrong, did she have any choice?

She showered and put on the only nightdress she could find, one she didn't even remember pushing into her bag. It consisted of a scrap of silk and peach lace, which Jarvis had purchased for her in Port Louis. She would have to get some more clothes before they went to Worton tomorrow. She would be forced to ask Jarvis for money. As she pulled the matching wrap, an equally scanty garment, over her bare shoulders, the invidiousness of her position struck her afresh. Jarvis might never miss the little he gave her, but she hated having nothing of her own. It seemed the less she took from him the better. It was she who should be the one to give.

On going back to the bedroom she heard him moving about in the dressing-room. The door between the two rooms was closed, but refusing to allow herself to hesitate she took a deep breath and knocked on it nervously. It was opened almost immediately by Jarvis, with a towel round his waist.

'Yes?' he asked, his face grimly enquiring.

Linsey's heart had been thudding and beat even faster at the sight of his broad, hair-covered chest. His chest was deep, his shoulders broad, and he looked suddenly too strong. She said, and immediately regretted saying it, 'You don't have to sleep in that small bed.'

After speaking she stared at him helplessly, thinking she must have a genius for thoughtless speech. She was really surpassing herself this evening, to her own detriment. Why couldn't she learn to use more charm, like Olivia James, for instance, instead of just bursting out with things?

Jarvis made no reply for several seconds. Because she was drawing short, deep breaths, she could smell the cleanliness of his skin, the warm male scent of him. There was a vein beating rapidly in his neck while a muscle jerked in his cheek.

Inscrutably he returned her stare. 'You're actually offering to share your bed, the big one in there?'

As his glance went past her shoulder in narrowed contemplation, she nodded numbly. Then he said harshly, 'If I accept your offer I might not want to sleep much. Just how far does your generosity extend? Last night I took. At least it began that way, but in the end you gave—and a lot more than I expected. You've changed, Linsey, we both have, but I don't want you regretting anything.'

'I'm offering you a good night's rest,' she stammered uncertainly. 'I think I must owe you a lot more . . .'

Folding his arms slowly across his middle, he looked down on her and snapped, 'You sound like a child who's been rehearsing for hours and still hasn't got it right.' His voice hardened. 'I'm ready to agree you owe me a lot, and it must be a step in the right direction that you admit it.'

His irony confused her. She was trying to be humble, but he wasn't helping her, neither was his disturbing nearness. Yet when she stepped backwards in nervous retreat, his hands came out to jerk her to him.

'You didn't really believe I was going to sleep in here by myself?' he asked bluntly.

Linsey's glance flew anxiously to his cold face. She didn't trust the glint in his eyes but told herself she had forfeited her right to object to anything. If this was to be her punishment, she must learn to submit without complaint. The light pressure of his firm lips on her own didn't seem too much like punishment, but immediately he touched her sensation began rioting through her entire body. She tingled to the fingertips she pressed against his chest with a protesting gasp, but she didn't struggle when he made no effort to release her. She could feel the strength of his arms as they tightened to render the fluttering motions of her hands ineffectual. In her ears she could hear the swift drumming of pulses, but she wasn't sure whether they were her own or his.

'I'm going to share your bed,' Jarvis muttered mockingly, but his voice was thick. His mouth, parted slightly, travelled down to the hollow of her throat and with a murmur of impatience he pushed the robe from her shoulders. Then he dealt just as ruthlessly with her delicate nightdress. Frantically she tried to stop him, suddenly terrified of her own growing excitement. She wanted to be a proper wife to him, to prove she was sorry for what she had done, but she didn't want to respond so eagerly that he would be aware of it and have another weapon to use against her.

She stiffened and tried to move away, but his hands clamped on her body so she couldn't escape. His mouth explored the rounded curves of her breast until she whimpered with ecstasy and clung to him blindly. She was fast losing all consciousness of her surroundings as everything disappeared in a sensuous cloud.

They clung together, so close that she was caught in the fire of his burning urgency. His hand slid down her back, fitting her to the hard contours of his body. Nor did he relax his hold when she cried out, but smothered her soft moans with sensual kisses she found impossible to resist. Her arms went around his neck as emotion ran riot between them. And, instead of protesting further, in a daze she heard herself saying breathlessly that she loved him.

'You want me to make love to you, you mean,' he taunted cynically.

When she tried to speak again, no sound issued through her numb lips. Taking her silence for consent, Jarvis picked her up with a savage exclamation, carrying her through to the other room, to crush her beneath him on the larger bed. Blindly she surrendered to a rapture which was sweeping her into seas where she had never ventured before. She hadn't wanted him to possess any part of her in hate, but her clamouring senses refused to deny him. Perhaps, too, this would be all she would have to remember, in the long, lonely years after he finally decided to discard her for ever. When his terrible desire for revenge began working the other way and wouldn't allow him to touch her.

The next morning, at breakfast, he told her he had

some business to attend to before they went to Worton. Because of this, she would have time to shop for any clothes she was going to need, and later they could all travel down together.

Linsey agreed, although she had never felt less like shopping in her life. A wave of homesickness for Mauritius, of all places, overwhelmed her. Or was it for the quiet, uncomplicated life she had led there? Certainly Harriet had been a tyrant, but she had never looked at her with such undisguised contempt as Jarvis did now.

She supposed she deserved all the censure she read in the green eyes that occasionally met hers during the course of their meal. This morning she even despised herself a little. Was it only an hour or two ago that she had shared so much passion in his arms? Bleakly she wondered why they were so aware of each other, why something between them, as uncomfortable as a flash of electricity, could flare in an instant, and instead of growing weaker, grow stronger, until it ignited a fire which threatened to burn them both up.

After breakfast she took Sean for a walk in the park, after which they had elevenses with his grandmother. Sean drank his glass of milk and told Linsey gravely about some of the things he had seen. He seemed very content with the flat and asked a lot of questions about London. Then he asked about Worton and if his grandmother was going there with them.

'No, young man,' she replied, and to Linsey, 'I rarely leave town these days, my dear, but I might join you for a weekend later.'

When Sean went to examine something at the other side of the huge drawing-room, she spoke again to Linsey. 'You don't know how happy I am to have a grandson, and to see you and Jarvis together again.'

Linsey smiled, nodding noncommittally, hoping desperately that Mrs Parradine would let the matter rest there. Unfortunately, she didn't. There followed questions, tactfully put, of course, which Linsey felt obliged to answer. Had Jarvis known his mother would be curious and deliberately left them alone? Mrs Parradine didn't ask anything very personal and she wasn't a petty woman. She merely wanted to know a little more about Linsey's life on Mauritius than Jarvis had told her. In a very short time Linsey felt her resentment fading, she even began to realise it was sometimes good to talk to someone.

She noticed that her mother-in-law didn't probe too deeply, nor was she inclined to criticise. In fact, Linsey was surprised at her tolerance. She hadn't had a chance to talk to her alone before now, but they seemed to learn quite a bit about each other in that brief hour before lunch. It would take a lot longer to get to know Mrs Parradine really well, Linsey thought wistfully, noting the same reserved pride in her as was in Jarvis.

She decided gratefully that Mrs Parradine was a fair woman, and this seemed confirmed when she said, 'One should never condemn another person, Linsey, for none of us is capable of reading someone else's mind.' She gave a brief, derisory laugh. 'Sometimes one is not always able to read one's own. Too many people judge from what they see, or what they think they see, and often jump to quite the wrong conclusions. I'm sure when you left Jarvis you had your reasons, which you, at least, believed were good ones, but I hope you won't ever do it again.'

Linsey swallowed and was very tempted to confess the whole story, but much as she was beginning to like Mrs Parradine she found it impossible to explain.

'Jarvis,' she got out with some difficulty, 'might be the one to leave this time.' She didn't try to pretend all was well between them. 'I hurt his pride, if nothing else, and to—a man,' she had been going to say Jarvis, 'this is all-important.'

'If it's only his pride that's hurt, my dear, he will eventually recover,' his mother observed shrewdly. 'Jarvis came to my room, this morning, before he left. He's delighted with his son, so proud of him. As so he should be, because Sean is a splendid little boy. Build on what you have, my dear, and perhaps soon everything will come all right.'

Linsey went shopping after lunch. Jarvis had said she should use the same stores where he had opened accounts for her when they were married. She only went to one and bought several articles very quickly, including a warm coat and mackintosh. It was raining as she came out, reminding her that she must get used to the English weather again. The mackintosh was a creamy beige, which the saleslady said looked wonderful with her fair hair and lightly tanned skin. Linsey also purchased three very simple evening dresses which would be suitable for the country. If Jarvis did ask her to act as his hostess in London, then she would have to shop for something more sophisticated.

When she returned to the flat she was surprised to find Jarvis there and was startled when he told her he had sent Sean and Miss Smith on ahead.

'To Worton?' Linsey exclaimed, as he relieved her of her parcels.

'He has to learn to do without you,' Jarvis nodded.

She looked at him, at his dark, handsome face, and felt angry. Then her anger faded as she remembered how she had deprived Jarvis of his son for four years. How could she complain at being parted from him for a few short hours? 'He's only small,' she sought to excuse her flare of indignation, 'and we've always been together.'

'Fine,' he retorted tersely. 'So you don't have to repeat everything you said when I sent him away in France.'

'No,' she agreed meekly, shrinking from his sarcasm,

'I'm sorry, Jarvis, for making such a fuss, especially when we're going to Worton ourselves. What time are we leaving?'

'Not today, anyway,' he drew her into the drawing-room as the butler came to close the door, 'I've decided we'll stay in London another night. My mother is dining out, but I thought we might go and have a look at the house.'

'The house?'

'Everything I say appears to be startling you, Linsey,' he observed drŷly. 'I've been away almost two months, you know. Perhaps I want to assure myself it hasn't fallen down in my absence.'

He was being sarcastic again, and again she tried to ignore it. She also also tried to hide her dismay at not being able to follow Sean to Worton, since she feared this might annoy Jarvis too.

'Is there any particular reason why you want to go to the house, apart from seeing that it's all right?'

'Actually, there is,' he admitted crisply. 'I've decided, while we're at Worton, to have some rooms prepared for Sean and Miss Smith. After I decide which, I'll contact a firm of interior decorators and tell them to get on with it.'

Linsey still didn't feel too happy about the arrangement when they went there after tea. She would love to have supervised the redecoration of Sean's rooms herself. On Mauritius she had often wished she had had a house of her own, where she might have prepared a proper nursery for Sean. Now, when she could have done so, it seemed she wasn't going to be given the opportunity.

'Wouldn't it be more fun,' she asked wistfully, as she followed Jarvis around the emptiness of the second floor, 'to do the job ourselves?'

'My dear girl,' he glanced at her coldly, 'I have neither the time nor the inclination.'

'I would love to do it,' she dared suggest.

'Leave it, Linsey,' he said. 'I believe in leaving things like this to the experts.'

So that was that. Linsey sighed despondently but didn't argue. How could she, anyway? She let the subject drop and only ventured a mild protest when Jarvis chose three rooms on the second floor, at the back of the house.

'Wouldn't it be better to have Sean nearer us? When Miss Smith has her evenings off, I should feel happier.'

'Well, I wouldn't,' Jarvis replied firmly. 'And when Miss Smith has time off one of the maids can take over. In any case, I don't expect we'll be here much.'

She was pleased about that, as the house evoked a lot of painful memories, many of which she would rather forget.

'Are you ready to go now?' she asked nervously, when he had made his final decision about the rooms. 'We promised your mother we wouldn't be late for dinner. I know she's going out, but she doesn't want the staff upset.'

'They're paid enough,' he snapped indifferently. 'I'd like you to look at our suite first, to see if you'd like to have it redone, while we're busy.'

Linsey didn't want to see it, but she knew she couldn't refuse to do as he asked. She was trembling as she entered the bedroom which Jarvis and she had used. It was impossible to believe it could be almost exactly as she had left it, but it was. Glancing around it, with wide, darkened eyes, she felt ill, and the extent of her anguish must have showed.

'You may well look devastated,' Jarvis rested taunting eyes on her face, holding her remorselessly to his side. 'This was where it all happened, wasn't it? Where you told me you were having a baby, and where you declared you'd lost it. Where you decided I was neglecting you for other women, and sought revenge by running away—depriving me of the child you swore you'd lost.'

Blindly she blinked back tears. Could she, in any way, justify her actions? 'I didn't do it for revenge, Jarvis. I'm sorry,' she whispered, her eyes pools of pain. 'I wish I could undo the past, but I can't. You do have Sean now, though, a son . . .'

'And I intend having others,' he interposed harshly when her voice choked on a sob. 'And you'll have no say in the matter, or their upbringing.'

Hurt flared through her until she trembled. 'You can only want me for one thing.'

His mirthless laughter rang above her head as he turned her to him. 'Don't sound so bitter, my dear. You ought to be thankful I want you at all, and you know very well that you're beginning to enjoy going to bed with me. We have this certain chemistry between us, which is even stronger than the hate we share, isn't it?'

CHAPTER TEN

LINSEY tried to appear indifferent, but failed to see how her light shrug didn't correspond with the clouded unhappiness in her eyes.

'I don't think this chemistry you talk about is all that strong,' she said.

'I don't agree,' Jarvis muttered grimly. 'I know you can make my heart race as no other woman can. Something, I assure you, I don't appreciate.'

'I'm sure you exaggerate,' she whispered, trembling under the intensity of his glance.

He jerked her to him, thrusting her hand hard against the front of the light shirt he wore. 'Feel it,' he mocked.

Snatching her hand away as if she had been burnt, she cried, 'I'm sure it doesn't bother you all that much. It can only be physical, anyway. It's not as though you cared for me.'

He watched her carefully, his face devoid of all expression. 'I take it our hate is mutual?'

'Not on my side,' she confessed, feeling suddenly too despairing to care how much he knew. 'I don't know if I loved you before, Jarvis, but I do now, very much.'

'You expect me to believe you?' he asked shortly, his face paling with what she took to be contempt.

'I'd like you to try to.' Her blue eyes misted sadly. Where was her pride? She wondered why it didn't seem to matter any more.

'It's your body I'm interested in,' he replied harshly, 'not your so-called love.'

'You'll soon tire if that's all,' she began, breaking off

as he drew her roughly into his arms.

'I don't think I'll ever tire of this,' he muttered as his mouth closed over hers.

Linsey tried to fight, the hurt in her heart too deep to be erased by the instant passion that flooded her every time Jarvis touched her.

'Please, Jarvis,' she whispered, desperately evading his sensuous lips. 'Your mother—our dinner . . .'

'To hell with dinner,' he said harshly, his arms tightening as he picked her up and strode towards the bed.

They left for Worton in the late afternoon of the following day. Jarvis had gone out again that morning leaving Linsey sleeping, a drugged sleep for which her body cried out. It was late when he had brought her back to the flat the previous evening. They remained in their own house a long time and Linsey, though reluctant to stay there, had hoped vaguely that they might have laid a few ghosts. The expression on Jarvis's face, however, when they came to leave, had told her indisputably that nothing had changed.

When they returned to the flat Mrs Parradine hadn't been long in from her dinner party. She looked reproachful but hadn't actually said anything. They had all had coffee and talked a little before going to bed. Jarvis had again shared the big double bed with Linsey, but as soon as he got in he had turned his back on her, without even saying goodnight. She had cried silently into her pillow until she fell asleep.

It was seven before they reached Worton. Sean, they were told by the manservant who opened the door to them, was already in bed. It dismayed Linsey that she didn't know where to find him. She had only been here once before, on that never-to-be-forgotten occasion when Jarvis had first kissed her. There hadn't been an opportunity to come again before the wedding, and afterwards so much had happened so quickly that she had almost forgotten about it.

Gazing at the old house, nestling snugly in the trees, as they drove towards it along the drive, she had had a great sense of homecoming. She was sad that the future was so uncertain, but decided she would try to live a day at a time and be content with what she had. At Worton she would discover again the English seasons. Spring, with its showers, the first fresh greenness. Summer, with its sunny brightness and warmth, the tantalising promise of long, hot days to come. Autumn, the richness of it, then winter. Sometimes she used to think she liked winter best, the evenings drawing in and log fires, frost and the dazzling whiteness of snow. More often than not it rained continually, but the dream was always there. And Christmas—it always arrived, no matter what the weather. She had missed the traditional English Christmas while she had been away. This year she hoped she would be spending it with Jarvis and Sean, and perhaps Mrs Parradine if she could be persuaded to leave London.

She was still gazing at the house intently as they drew up beside it. Close at hand, it seemed even more benign and mellow than it had looked from a distance. It wasn't over-large, but it tended to ramble a little. Many of the rooms weren't used and Jarvis kept only a skeleton staff.

'I could help out,' Linsey had suggested eagerly, on the way down. 'It would give me something to do.'

'I won't have my wife working,' Jarvis had squashed the idea sharply. 'If extra help is needed there are plenty of local people who would be glad of a job.'

'Wouldn't that seem extravagant in times like these?' she protested.

He glanced at her coldly. 'It can't be bad to provide employment for someone, and I pay good wages.'

Linsey hadn't said anything more. It wouldn't be

good to take a job from someone who really needed it, but she couldn't imagine how she was going to fill in her days. She would hate having nothing to do. It might have been different if Jarvis had offered some companionship, but as he didn't even like her she couldn't rely on him. Eventually he might be willing to let her do some voluntary work, if she was patient. Meanwhile, she and Sean could get to know the house and explore the countryside. Jarvis couldn't possibly stop her from doing that.

The manservant followed them upstairs with their luggage. Jarvis took Linsey to a room at the front of the house and threw the two pieces of luggage he was carrying on the bed.

'That will be all, Dick,' he dismissed the man, who was staring at Linsey curiously.

'You'd better learn to be more correct with the staff,' he said shortly, as the door closed. 'On the yacht, in London, now here. They can't take their eyes off you. Do you think I haven't noticed?'

Jarvis's eyes were hard and cold as they rested on her flushed face. 'That's hardly my fault,' she protested.

He continued as if she had never spoken. 'The men I employ are very circumspect. It must be the way you look at them. I'd advise you to be more prudent with my friends.'

Linsey nodded, feeling too near tears to quarrel with him about it. In the savage mood he appeared to be in, she would only lose any argument anyway. She deemed it wiser to concentrate her attention on the bedroom. It was large and airy with the usual bathroom leading off. The carpet, a soft green, toned with the cover on the huge double bed and the furniture was old and mellow. It was obviously a man's room, but she liked it.

Jarvis seemed suddenly as willing as she to leave the

question of her indiscretion alone. 'There's a suite next door,' he said abruptly, 'that we can occupy if you like.'

'I'd as soon stay here,' she replied.

'You may find it rather cramped.' As he glanced around, his hands came out automatically to relieve her of the jacket she was wearing. As his fingers brushed the bare skin of her neck, his expression changed and darkened. 'Are you going to bath and rest before dinner?'

Her senses leapt, she felt her heart begin to thump violently. She knew she had only to nod her head and she would be in his arms, whether in the bath or out of it. His hands were already curving over her shoulders towards her breasts. It wasn't until she felt the unforgiving cruelty in them that she was jerked to the full reality of what she was inviting.

'No,' she gasped, twisting from him, 'I won't have time. Didn't Dick say dinner was at eight?'

'You appear to have an obsession with meals,' he snapped.

'I'm hungry,' she lied, relieved that he didn't follow her as she stumbled to the window. 'Is-isn't the view wonderful?' she stammered. 'I-I'm going to enjoy exploring all this with Sean. Jarvis,' she rushed on, talking to the glass, wishing her thudding pulses would calm down, 'I'd like to go and see him before I change.'

'You'll see him tomorrow.' He stood very still, watching her. 'I have to return to town tomorrow, unfortunately. While I'm away I don't want you taking Sean out on your own. Let him learn to be with other people.'

'You mean teach him to do without me?'

'If you want to put it that way, yes.' He took no notice of the bitter whiteness in her face as she swung back to him. 'While you're here you won't take him anywhere. If he's invited out, Miss Smith will go with him, if I'm not available.'

'But—surely, just for a walk? I mean . . .' Linsey was stammering again, but she didn't seem able to help it.

'No!' he rasped, as though violently angry. 'You may not. And if you disobey me, Linsey, I'll force you to live in London and leave Sean here.'

'You wouldn't!' she cried hoarsely, suddenly trembling. 'You couldn't be so cruel?'

'Try me.' He seemed to enjoy seeing the trembling she couldn't disguise. 'I think it's about time you suffered a little.'

Linsey tried to understand but failed. It wasn't difficult to understand what she had done to Jarvis's pride, but wicked and mistaken as she had been to leave him, she was sure it wasn't bad enough to justify the way he treated her during the following weeks. His harshness was something she tried desperately to ignore, for at least short periods, but eventually her unhappiness began affecting her physically until some mornings she woke up feeling quite ill.

Jarvis never had anything more to do with her than he could help. He might share her bed, but if he ever touched her it was accidentally. He went to London more than he had said he would in the beginning, but he never took Linsey with him. Once, when she had asked him to take her so she might visit his mother, he had refused.

He had told her his mother wasn't well and when she enquired what was wrong, he said nothing serious.

Linsey had stared at him anxiously. 'Why doesn't she come to Worton for a while? The country air would do her good and she must be longing to see Sean.'

'She'll come when she's ready,' he had replied, forbidding Linsey to get in touch with her.

He seemed able to read her mind, just as easily as he

imposed his will over her. He forbade her to ring his mother, and she wondered if he had forbidden Mrs Parradine to ring his wife. Linsey couldn't imagine Mrs Parradine obeying such instructions, but Jarvis might have told her anything. He was bitter and harsh these days, enough to frighten even a woman as resolute and fearless as his mother.

Linsey spent a lot of time walking. If the people in the neighbourhood wondered why she was out so much on her own, no one ever said anything to her, and for this she was grateful. She was always frightened that if any speculation regarding her wanderings came to Jarvis's ears, he would somehow prevent her from going out again. The thought of having to spend her time confined to the house, with nothing to do, was almost more than she could bear.

She didn't dare see too much of Sean. Miss Smith, she was aware, was vaguely but not unduly puzzled by her apparently unnatural behaviour. She had worked for other mothers who had shown little real interest in their offspring. Sometimes, though, when sensing Miss Smith's unspoken criticism, Linsey would forget to be cautious and take Sean for a glorious ramble in the fields and woods. Unfortunately Jarvis came home early one day, and caught her.

They had gone farther afield than usual. Sean was tired and dirty and sleeping in her arms when Jarvis found them. She was sitting on the edge of a grassy gutter, holding Sean tightly, her cheek against the top of his head, just letting him sleep, when Jarvis found them.

Sean was immediately snatched from her, and Jarvis had been furious. 'You little bitch!' he had snapped, taking care not to waken his son, letting his black, glittering eyes convey his fury. 'After this I won't tell you again. Disobey my orders once more and you'll go to London!'

When his mother did ring and ask Linsey to visit her in town and bring Sean, she didn't know what to say. She had come to believe, when Mrs Parradine made no attempt to get in touch with her, that Jarvis must have told her not to. Now, as it became obvious that he had done nothing of the sort, she was bewildered. How could she refuse Mrs Parradine's invitation without telling her the truth? How did you tell a woman that her son kept his wife more or less a prisoner? Mrs Parradine probably wouldn't believe it, anyway, and why should she? Jarvis was self-assertive and dominant, but apart from an occasional slight impatience was always very kind to his mother. His mother loved him, his staff did too, and, seeing him with Sean, Linsey knew they considered him a devoted father. She also knew they didn't blame him for the apparent rift in his marriage. They liked Linsey, but as she had left him, the fault must be hers.

Linsey thought fast as she clutched the receiver in nervous hands.

'Are you there?' Mrs Parradine asked sharply.

'Yes.' Linsey went clammy all over with apprehension but forced herself to go on. 'I'll bring Sean tomorrow, Mrs Parradine, but only if you'll promise not to mention it to Jarvis. You see, he doesn't approve of either of us coming to London. I know Sean might tell him afterwards, but Jarvis won't blame him.'

'But I thought Jarvis might bring you!'

Mrs Parradine seemed taken aback. Linsey said hastily, 'We'll come by train. Sean's never been on a train before. He's sure to love it.'

Sean did. The mid-morning train was far from full and he practically danced with excitement. Linsey, drunk on recklessness, gave Miss Smith the whole day off. Jarvis might murder her, but at least she was going to have Sean for a few hours to herself first.

Mrs Parradine, recovering well from a severe attack

of rheumatism, was delighted to see them. She thought Sean was thriving, but was aghast over Linsey. 'You're far too thin, child—you look terrible!'

Linsey flushed, parrying such frank remarks as best as she could, and felt happier when Mrs Parradine, with a sigh, turned to Sean again.

'As you'll know,' she said obliquely, 'Jarvis comes to see me sometimes. He doesn't look well, either. Nor is his temper so good. I would say he's a man under a considerable strain.'

'He works too hard,' Linsey managed.

'He has always worked hard,' Mrs Parradine snorted inelegantly, 'but I've never seen him so haggard as he is now, not since you first left him.'

Despite what had been an uneasy beginning, Linsey enjoyed being with her mother-in-law. So did Sean. Too soon it was time to go, but Mrs Parradine promised to pay them a visit as soon as she was able to. The butler came to say their taxi was waiting and they said goodbye. As they left the house, Linsey was startled to see another taxi drawing up and Olivia James getting out.

'Why, hello!' Olivia smiled maliciously, on catching sight of Linsey with Sean. 'If it isn't the little runaway bride!'

'Good afternoon, Miss James,' Linsey replied stiffly. 'I'm sorry, we've a train to catch.'

'A train?' Olivia's pencilled brows rose. 'I've just had lunch with Jarvis and he didn't say anything about a train. In fact, when he asked me to call and see his mother—who might, incidentally, be my mother-in-law soon—he didn't even mention that you were here.'

'Perhaps he forgot.' Better the humiliation of that than to let Olivia suspect he hadn't known. 'Sean had never been on a train before and I—I mean, we—thought it would be a nice treat.'

'Really?'

As Olivia's brows threatened to disappear, Linsey almost dived towards her taxi. 'I really must go now, Miss James.'

All the way back to Worton Olivia's words danced through Linsey's head. Lunch with Jarvis, calling on his mother. Jarvis hadn't been telling the truth. He must intend getting a divorce, after all. He had said he wouldn't, but that was probably just to fool Linsey until he made sure of getting Sean. He never touched her now, so clearly hating her that she might have guessed! All the signs were there, only she had been fool enough to believe him.

It was after nine before Jarvis arrived home that evening. Linsey had known he had a business dinner and had hoped he might decide to stay in town. She had just finished having a bath when he strode into the bedroom. The journey to London, combined with the tensions of the day, had tired her, so rather than dress again, she had just put on a light wrap, having decided to go straight to bed.

Apprehensively she swung round as he entered the room. It was obvious from the look on his face that he knew where she had been, and her heart sank.

'So!' he snapped, making no attempt to disguise his blazing anger. 'You've been to London, disobeying me again, but farther afield this time?'

She tried to stop shaking at the impact of his smouldering gaze. 'Your mother asked me to bring Sean to see her.'

'You didn't tell me.'

'Only because I feared you wouldn't let me go if I did.'

'You know damned well I wouldn't have let you go!' He ripped of his jacket and flung it on a chair, the violence of his mood frightening Linsey half out of her wits. The anger in his eyes leapt as he covered the distance between them in seconds. Grasping the brush with which she had been brushing her long golden hair, he threw it aside as he jerked her to her feet. Then ruthlessly he shook her.

'I'm sorry, Jarvis,' her voice broke on a sob as she stared up at him, her head reeling.

'You are?' he spoke coldly. 'I don't see much sign of it. You wouldn't have told me. I'd never have known if Olivia hadn't given me a ring.'

So that was how he'd found out! She might have guessed. She tried to clear her throat. 'I didn't expect to be able to keep it from you. Sean would have told you, or your mother, so I was going to tell you myself, tonight or in the morning.'

'Which doesn't alter the fact that initially you set out to deceive me,' he retorted, between his teeth.

Linsey looked at him with anxious, defensive blue eyes. 'Sometimes you drive me to deceiving you, Jarvis. You hate me so much, and lately you've even seemed to dislike touching me.'

'And that's bothered you, has it?' he taunted, his eyes hardening with mocking intent as he began dragging her towards the bed.

'No, Jarvis, no!' she pleaded desperately, her heart racing out of control as she guessed his intentions.

As she held back, he lifted her, flinging her across the green bedspread and coming down brutally on top of her. She hated the way he hurt her, but she hated more the hot rush of awareness which swept through her veins.

For a minute they lay there, the breath knocked out of them. 'Jarvis, if you don't let me go you'll regret it,' Linsey heard herself moaning. 'Olivia said——'

'Shut up!' he cut in savagely, his breath rasping as he threw off his remaining clothing. 'I don't want to hear about her or anyone else. Talking never made any impression on you, why should you think it might on me? I should have tried a different kind of discipline.'

'Oh, no . . .!' As she twisted from the cruelty of hands that rapidly stripped her naked, her voice shook, but he merely pulled her against his hard body, his mouth bruising, using undisguised force, as though determined to subdue her.

She was trembling in earnest now, shuddering beneath the impact of his harsh kisses, while trying to fight the rising tide of her own urgent desires. They were both fighting this passionate need of each other which always succeeded in drawing them together. Instinctively Linsey knew he was having as great a struggle as she was, but this didn't help. It was no comfort to sense that he wanted her but despised himself for it.

'Jarvis, won't you listen to me?' she whispered huskily.

'No,' the green eyes flashed as he lowered his head and his mouth moved over her exposed skin. 'Why should I listen to you when I think you've missed this as much as I have?'

The derision in his voice was reflected in the hard, caressing movements of hands that bruised as they explored, but eventually the spinning, floating sensation he was producing had her murmuring incoherently in his arms as a sense of enchantment began filling her.

His mouth forced her trembling lips apart and his possessive hands slid over her lurching stomach to find her breasts. 'You drive me mad,' he said thickly. 'I mean to have you, Linsey, you may as well give in.'

'No,' she moaned, but her voice lacked conviction.

'Then I'll have to make you,' he rasped.

Linsey resisted for a moment, uncertain and shaken, but the hard pressure of his limbs on hers, the deliberately arousing touch of his hands, the sensuous passion of his mouth all combined to demolish her defences against him. She heard him gasp as his body moved in over hers and was helpless to stop him.

Momentarily she fought the darkness that threatened at his ruthless possession, then suddenly she wasn't frightened any more. Jarvis might be taking her in anger, but if he wanted her she didn't mind which way. She loved him so much this couldn't be wrong. Tightly she wound her arms around his neck, wanting to give herself completely. The heavy rasp of his breathing, the excitement she could feel mounting within him, only brought an urgent desire to respond. As his arms tightened she found she was clinging to him, whispering his name passionately against his demanding lips, again and again.

Afterwards, when he left her, she tried to sleep, but couldn't. What a fool she had been to think this past hour would make any difference! As Jarvis closed the door sharply, all her new hopes died within her. He said he would sleep in the suite next door and not disturb her again. He had sounded so final, she cried, but an hour later, she lay dry-eyed and shocked. It was as if the unbearable pain she had felt when he had left her had torn a veil from her mind, showing her, for the first time, things about herself which she had never really understood. She couldn't believe she could have been so blind!

For the first time she saw herself and her marriage in a new way. If, at the start, Jarvis had grown a little impatient, she had been too young to understand that his impatience had sprung from his increasing need of what she had consistently withheld from him. She hadn't been so young in years as in experience, and this had worried her continually. She had been terrified of boring him. But instead of speaking openly about the uncertainties that beset her, she had been too proud to confess that she wasn't nearly as confident as he thought she was. He had wanted her overwhelmingly and she had been frightened. Hadn't she grabbed at every excuse to avoid giving herself completely? She had even tried to turn her parents' death to her own advantage, with this in mind. Her grief had been real enough, but she had deliberately exaggerated it in order to appeal to Jarvis's sympathy, to keep him out of her bed.

If she had used some common sense and learned to accept her extremely sensuous nature, their honeymoon would have been vastly different. She had had a crazy idea that Jarvis wanted a lady for his wife and that ladies didn't get carried away by—that kind of thing. The pressures she had put on him, she saw now, must have been well nigh unendurable. Then, their harrowing return to London with his passion still unslaked and burning at fever heat, and she still asking the impossible of him. He had tried desperately hard to respect her desire to be chaste in mourning, while she had been too muddled up to even think straight. When she had discovered she was pregnant, instead of being delighted, she had merely indulged in a further flood of self-pity. She had only herself to blame that Jarvis's affection had grown noticeably cooler and the rift between them had widened daily. Had she really gone to his office that day to rejoice with him about not having lost the baby? Somehow she doubted it. It was more likely that she had simply intended using the baby as an excuse to regain his attention and sympathy.

She had been an only child and her parents had spoiled her. It was a wonder she wasn't entirely selfish. She was grateful that the repercussions of that spoiling hadn't gone so deep she was unable to see where she had gone wrong. It must be too late now, of course, to convince Jarvis she had changed, but at least she could do something to undo the harm she had done. She must go away, leave him to find happiness with someone else. He might believe she was sorry, if she tried to explain, but that wouldn't bring back the love she had destroyed. And she couldn't bear to live with him without it.

It was almost midnight when she stole from the house and set off in the direction of the nearest town. The station was five miles away and there she hoped to catch an early train which would take her to London. From London she would ring Jarvis, she had already left him a note explaining that she wasn't coming back, and why, but she would give him a ring, just to make sure.

It was a fine night and she wore a pair of sensible shoes, as she didn't expect to get a lift. At this time of night, in these parts, there was very little traffic. As she covered mile after mile, the road was so quiet she became absorbed in unhappy thoughts, and almost jumped out of her skin when a car did pull up beside her.

'I'm sorry——' she was about to refuse the invitation before it was ever issued, when, suddenly aghast, she realised it was Jarvis.

He flung open the door, catching her arm even as she turned to flee, pulling her into the car, into his arms, slamming the door shut again. 'My God, Linsey!' his tortured groan was muffled against her hair. 'Never—never do this to me again!'

The shock of Jarvis's arrival stunned her. She couldn't think of a thing to say. Clinging to him as though he was the only solid thing on earth, she gasped, 'How did you know I'd gone? How did you find me?'

'I found your note,' his voice was still hoarse. 'I couldn't stand it any longer. I love you, and it was killing me, treating you the way I was doing. I was torturing both of us and I went to your room to ask you to forgive me. When I found you'd gone I nearly went crazy. It was worse than when you went to Mauritius.'

Her cheek was against his, she was crushed in his arms, she could feel almost every bit of him, yet what he was telling her seemed to have no reality. 'You can't possibly love me, Jarvis,' she whispered brokenly, 'not after everything I've done!'

The flash of approaching headlights brought from Jarvis an impatient, smothered oath. He released her reluctantly to pull on to a piece of waste land at the side of the road and almost before she was aware he had moved she was fast in his arms again.

He put gentle fingers under her chin, lifting it so he could kiss her mouth. It was a long kiss, without passion but full of tenderness and warmth. 'I love you, darling,' he brushed her last words aside, daring her to question the adoration in his eyes, 'I think I always have. I know I always will.'

'I know I love you,' she said in shaken tones, almost unable to comprehend that she was here, in Jarvis's arms, and he was telling her something she had never expected to hear.

'You really love me?' he queried, something very like worship in his glance. 'You said you did, but I couldn't believe you meant it.'

'Jarvis,' she touched his face with a wondering hand, seeing the darkness in his eyes as she did so, feeling the hard tremors under his skin, 'I'm not sure what I felt in the past, but a long time ago I realised I loved you, only I was still too frightened of my emotions to admit how much. When,' she hesitated, scarcely daring to ask, 'when did you first know you loved me?'

His arms tightened, his hands caressing her back, slipping through her soft hair. 'It might be wiser to begin at the beginning,' he smiled grimly. 'I saw you, I wanted you, and what I wanted I always made sure I got. On our honeymoon, when you persisted in withholding part of yourself from me, you drove me almost to madness. You blew hot and cold so consistently, I often felt more like strangling you than loving you. Yet, for all that, I found it very hard to restrain myself whenever I had you in my arms. I began to believe you hadn't been ready for marriage, but I knew you were far from cold by nature. And there was this spark between us, an ever-recharging surge of electricity, which convinced me we could find a kind of earthly paradise together, if only you would learn to trust me.

'Even in London,' he continued harshly, 'when you were grieving for your parents, I understood how you felt, but it didn't prevent me wanting you. When you so obviously didn't want me, I had to leave you alone completely. You were so lovely and desirable, I knew I couldn't hope to keep to half measures. Then, when you learnt about the baby and didn't seem to want it, I didn't know what to think.'

'Oh, Jarvis,' her eyes blurred with tears, dampening his shirt as he held her face against his shoulder, 'I shouldn't have blamed you . . .'

'Well,' his mouth quirked with a brief flicker of humour, 'I'd have felt worse if you'd blamed someone else.' His tone changing tautly, he said, 'I was annoyed with myself that I hadn't given you more time, yet when we thought you'd lost the baby I was devastated. I wanted you both, you see, and it appeared I'd lost you both.'

It took courage to lift her head and look at him, but she managed it. 'What happened was more my fault than yours, Jarvis. I was a spoiled brat. I only considered myself, never you. I never stopped to look at things from your point of view.' Her voice shook, but she was determined to tell him how she had seen herself earlier that evening and wouldn't let him interrupt. And, as she finished and his arms tightened again, instead of pushing her contemptuously away, she felt an aching sense of relief which encouraged her to make the final, vital confession.

'When I learnt I was still pregnant, Jarvis, I rushed to your office to tell you, and found you with Olivia James in your arms. It was a terrible shock, but if I'd been more adult I'd never have flown to Mauritius the way I did. I thought my heart was breaking, but I suspect it was more a case of hurt pride and a desire for revenge that drove me to act as I did.'

'You saw me with Olivia?' he frowned, 'Oh, God, if only I'd known! She was just off to America for a couple of years and I was so delighted, I obliged when she asked me to kiss her goodbye. For me, it didn't mean a thing. She was married then, anyway. If only you'd waited,' he groaned, 'I could have explained!'

'Would you?'

'I don't know ... Maybe we both had too much pride. I'm not sure,' he admitted frankly, 'what I would have done. I know that when you disappeared and I couldn't find you, I tried to tell myself I was well rid of you and needn't feel guilty about associating with other women. Only I spent more time thinking of you and what I would do to you if I ever caught up with you again than I did of them. It made me even more furious when I discovered I found no pleasure in the company of other women any more. I might have pretended I had, when I met you, but there was no one. I didn't realise how bitter I was becoming, and when I did it seemed too late to do anything about it.'

'You don't have to explain.' Linsey heard the agony in his voice and put gentle fingers over his lips to stop him, but he simply kissed her fingers, one by one, then went on, as if he had to.

'When I saw you again, standing on that beach on Mauritius, I could scarcely believe my eyes, and all I could think of was revenge. I was going to make you suffer, if it was the last thing I did! I was curious when you seemed abnormally frightened at the sight of me.

I'd expected you to be surprised, but not that much, and it became even more interesting when I realised you were hiding something. I thought it must be another man, and when I discovered it was Sean I was stunned—and angrier than I could ever remember being in my life.'

'I thought you'd left the island,' Linsey faltered, as he paused, feeling a tremor run through her even to recall the incidents he was describing.

'No,' he sighed against the top of her head. 'I knew I couldn't leave you; all I did was pretend to. When I took you to have lunch on the yacht, then down to my cabin to see how desperate you were to get home, I knew I could never let you go again. I nearly made love to you that day—I'll never know how I managed to resist you. When I did find out about Sean, the anger and hate was still there, but there was also tremendous joy. I could have murdered you for keeping him from me, though.'

'I thought you would take him away,' Linsey reiterated unhappily, and Jarvis said quickly, 'I know, Linsey, and you were right to be apprehensive. I meant to. I was delighted with my son, so much so that it seemed incredible that soon my most prevalent feelings were those of jealousy. And I was actually jealous of your love for him, not his for you. It began to drive me mad. You didn't love me, you loved him. On the yacht, on the way back here, when you responded so ardently that night in your cabin, I believed it was basically sex. That was when I began to get the idea that if I could keep you and Sean apart you might learn to love me. It got so bad I couldn't bear to see you near him, loving him, smiling at him, ignoring me. It became as if I had a wild beast in my breast that wouldn't listen to reason.'

'Jarvis,' Linsey steadied her voice with a deep breath, 'I love you quite desperately, and what I feel for you is quite different from the love I have for Sean.'

'I know, my darling,' Jarvis murmured huskily. 'It's the same with me, only he had your love, whatever kind it was, while I seemed to have nothing. Yet tonight, when I thought you'd gone again, I was ready to grovel. I didn't care if you hated me any more, just as long as I found you and you agreed to stay. When I saw you walking along the road I was so thankful I was ready to agree to any terms you cared to dictate.'

She looked at him, meeting his intent, glittering gaze, letting him see the love in her eyes. 'I don't want terms,' she said, 'I just want you. But I thought you only wanted Sean, that's why I decided to leave and let you have him. You see, I thought you hadn't been telling me the truth—when I saw Olivia . . .'

'Where did you meet her?' he cut in harshly.

'As we were leaving your mother's. She said she'd had lunch with you, and she hinted . . .'

'Spare me,' he cut in again. 'Darling, I haven't seen Olivia since the day we left France. Today I had lunch with a business colleague on the south coast and a business dinner in London. And it was all male. Not even a secretary in sight!'

Suddenly Linsey didn't care about Olivia or any other woman. She loved Jarvis and they were together, nothing else mattered. They had each other—and Sean.

'Forgive me,' she whispered, 'for doubting you.'

'If you'll forgive me for the last weeks?'

'Let's forget about them,' she begged, her arms slipping around his neck.

'If you're sure, my love?' Jarvis's own arms tightened and he said unsteadily, 'We have Sean and I hope we'll have other children, but nothing really matters but you.'

She moved restlessly against him, feeling drunk on

the passion in his voice. As she nodded, his mouth descended to find her lips. He kissed her hungrily while his hands stroked gently along her shoulders to find the pulse beating hard in her throat. The shared sweetness of their kisses helped to banish all the pain they had suffered, and, as Jarvis murmured loving endearments in her ears, Linsey clung to him feverishly, whispering his name. He kissed her again, almost reverently, holding her close, and she had never suspected she might feel as happy as she did then.

Eventually he stirred, drawing back from the growing temptation of her mouth, but with a look of increasing urgency in his eyes. 'I love you,' he said, thickly, wryly, 'but there must be better places!' Then suddenly he was smiling, adoring her. 'Shall we go home, my darling wife?'

'Yes,' she whispered, 'let's,' but before he switched the ignition, she kissed him again, very softly and lovingly.

As they drove back to Worton she snuggled up against him and his arm held her firmly to his side. It was lovely to go home, Linsey thought dreamily, but she wouldn't really mind where they went, as long as they were together.

Harlequin Plus
A WORD ABOUT THE AUTHOR

Margaret Pargeter's earliest memories are of her childhood in Northumberland, in northern England. World War II was raging, but in spite of the gravity of the times, she recalls, people always tried to find something to smile about. That memory, and that philosophy, have stayed with her through the years.

Short-story writing was a habit that began in her early teens, and after her marriage she wrote serials for a newspaper. When her children were in school she did several years of market research, which she believes gave her a greater insight about people and their problems, insight that today helps her in creating interesting plots and developing believable characters.

Today, Margaret lives in a small house in the quiet Northumbrian valley where she grew up. On the subject of writing romances, she is convinced of one thing: "It is not easy. But not the least among my blessings is the pleasure I get from knowing that people enjoy reading my books."

The bestselling epic saga of the Irish.
An intriguing and passionate story
that spans 400 years.

FIRST...
The Defiant

Lady Elizabeth Hatton, highborn
Englishwoman, was not above using
her position to get what she wanted
...and more than anything in the
world she wanted Rory
O'Donnell, the fiery Irish rebel.
But it was an alliance that promised
only ruin....

THEN...
The Survivors

Against a turbulent background of
political intrigue and royal
corruption, the determined,
passionate Shanna O'Hara searched
for peace in her beloved
but troubled Ireland. Meanwhile
in England, hot-tempered
Brenna Coke fought against
a loveless marriage....

What the press says about Harlequin romance fiction...

"When it comes to romantic novels...
Harlequin is the indisputable king."
—*New York Times*

" 'Harlequin [is]... the best and the biggest.' "
—*Associated Press* (quoting Janet Dailey's husband, Bill)

"The most popular reading matter of
American women today."
—*Detroit News*

"... exciting escapism, easy reading, interesting
characters and, always, a happy ending....
They are hard to put down."
—*Transcript-Telegram*. Holyoke (Mass.)

"... a work of art."
—*Globe & Mail*. Toronto